ChangelingPress.com

Roman/Brick Duet
A Bones MC Romance
Marteeka Karland

Roman/Brick Duet
A Bones MC Romance
Marteeka Karland

All rights reserved.
Copyright ©2023 Marteeka Karland

ISBN: 9781605218762

Publisher:
Changeling Press LLC
315 N. Centre St.
Martinsburg, WV 25404
ChangelingPress.com

Printed in the U.S.A.

Editor: Katriena Knights
Cover Artist: Marteeka Karland

The individual stories in this anthology have been previously released in E-Book format.

No part of this publication may be reproduced or shared by any electronic or mechanical means, including but not limited to reprinting, photocopying, or digital reproduction, without prior written permission from Changeling Press LLC.

This book contains sexually explicit scenes and adult language which some may find offensive and which is not appropriate for a young audience. Changeling Press books are for sale to adults, only, as defined by the laws of the country in which you made your purchase.

Table of Contents

Roman/Brick Duet 2
Roman (Iron Tzars MC 2) 4
   Chapter One 5
   Chapter Two 23
   Chapter Three 37
   Chapter Four 50
   Chapter Five 63
   Chapter Six 76
   Chapter Seven 85
   Epilogue 103
Brick (Iron Tzars MC 3) 108
   Chapter One 109
   Chapter Two 124
   Chapter Three 137
   Chapter Four 150
   Chapter Five 163
   Chapter Six 179
   Chapter Seven 191
   Chapter Eight 204
   Chapter Nine 219
Marteeka Karland 225
Changeling Press E-Books 226

Roman (Iron Tzars MC 2)
A Bones MC Romance
Marteeka Karland

Winter -- My life hasn't been easy. For so long, my sister has been the only one I could rely on. When we were teenagers our father sold us to sexual predators who hurt us. We both have the scars to prove it. But we were rescued, and I got revenge for both of us. That was over a decade ago. I love the home we found with Black Reign, but now it's time to move on. To live outside the cocoon the club wrapped us in. One man in particular calls to me on a primitive level. His name is Roman. And I want him for my own.

Roman -- I'm the enforcer for Iron Tzars. Violence is in the job description. Never thought I'd find myself attracted to a woman as fragile as Winter. She and her sister have been through a lot, but there's a core of iron in her. She's stronger than she looks, and the fight in her stirs the primitive Alpha male inside me. It's time I show her she's more than the sum of her scars. She's a friggin' *goddess*.

Chapter One
Roman

I'd never been so glad to leave a place behind as I cheerfully rolled out of Lake Worth, Florida. I did my part as enforcer for Iron Tzars, but the entire time we'd been there I felt like we were outgunned. Black Reign MC might not be a rival club, but they were by no means safe. As evidenced by the way they took care of business with the fucking men we'd caught taking orphans from the group home in the city.

Violence didn't bother me. If a motherfucker deserved it, there was no limit. My balls were twitching because of the casual ease with which that bastard, Chief, had taken the skin off the men he tortured. Yeah, Brick had participated, but our VP was emotionless on the best of days. Chief and El Diablo were different. I wouldn't say they enjoyed the act, but I wouldn't say they didn't, either. It hadn't *bothered* them in the least.

But what *really* had me glad to see this place in my rear view were the twin women who haunted the place like ghosts. Eerily lovely, they always seemed to be where I was. Neither said anything, but they stared at me constantly. More than one of Black Reign's members gave me the stink-eye over it, too though no one would tell me why. Only that I should stay away from them. I didn't even know the pair's names, for fuck's sake! Didn't *want* to know!

I drove the Bronco we'd taken as a chase vehicle down to Lake Worth. Normally I'd ride my bike with the other brothers, but someone had to drive the big thing back to Evansville. As Road Captain, the task would normally fall to Clutch, but he'd had a family emergency and had headed back early. After that, I'd drawn the short straw. My bike was stowed in the trailer, and here I was. Behind the wheel of a fucking cage.

Lost in thought, my eyes on the road as my brothers surrounded the cage in front and behind, I reached over and switched on the radio. I had no desire to dwell on another club. Not even one our former president -- and my long-time friend -- now belonged to. I was an enforcer in Iron Tzars. Not Sergeant at Arms. I didn't need to find trouble, only punish it. Besides, if Sting -- our current president and son to the former president -- had decided Warlock had to be killed for his infractions against the club, I would be responsible for carrying out the sentence. I didn't want to do that. It looked like El Diablo had forestalled anything in that regard, though I had no idea why. It was rare for anyone to leave the Iron Tzars. When they did, the situation was permanent. Warlock was only the second man I knew of not to die when he left or was asked to leave. Oh, well. Above my paygrade. I was just thankful I didn't have to kill my brother.

A tap on my shoulder had my head whipping around. When I saw that same eerily lovely face I'd been trying not to think about right next to mine, I was so startled I jerked the wheel. The girl squealed and disappeared from my immediate vision.

"What the fuck?" The Bronco hit the rumble strips on the shoulder. My tires must have squealed, because several of the riders in front of us either glanced over their shoulder or turned their head slightly to look in their mirrors. They moved to the center lane in case I was out of control. When I slowed and pulled fully onto the shoulder, they followed.

I got as far over as I could but didn't turn on my

flashers. Though we weren't hauling any contraband, I'd rather not enlist the help of a good Samaritan or, God forbid, the state police.

Once stopped, I put the thing in park and turned around. "What the everlasting, God forsaken fuck are you doing in my fuckin' vehicle?" I growled at the girl but tried not to yell. I got the feeling she was fragile and, though I was angry, I didn't want to scare her. As I spoke, the other one poked her head from behind the backseat in the cargo area. "Shoulda guessed. You two ain't ever far apart." There was a knock at my window, saving the girls from a lecture.

Instead of rolling down the window, I opened the door and stepped out. The two girls ducked back behind the seat, the first one having returned to what had probably been their hiding place in my fucking Bronco.

"You good?" Brick peered inside the vehicle, looking for a threat. His hand was on the gun at his hip, but he didn't draw.

"Yeah. Just realized I had a couple of stowaways."

Brick raised an eyebrow. Instead of explaining, I walked him around to the back and opened the tail door for him to see for himself. They were hiding behind cargo, but both of them poked their heads up when I opened the door so I could see their eyes and the top of their heads over their hiding place.

"Fuck." He scrubbed a hand over his face. "You two in trouble?"

One of them shook her head. The other girl shrank back.

"You know you can't stay with us. We'll have to take you back."

"No." The braver of the two shook her head. "We

want to stay with you."

"You afraid to go back?" Brick crossed big arms over his brawny chest. "They hurt you?"

Black Reign didn't seem like the type of club to hurt women. They were protective as all get out of any of the women under their care, especially these two. The idea that any woman might be running from that club didn't sit well with me, but the thought that either of these women had an issue with them made me want to drive back and beat the fuck out of someone.

"No," she said in a soft voice. "It was time to leave."

I looked at Brick. "We're only an hour from home. We could let Black Reign know once we get back to the clubhouse."

"Let me check with Sting. He may know something we don't. If not, he'll decide what to do."

"Can we please stop at a gas station or something?" The braver one raised her head farther as she spoke. "It's why I bothered you. We need a bathroom break."

"You shoulda said something before now," I groused. "We've been on the fuckin' road for twelve fuckin' hours! Stopped twice! Why didn't you get out then?"

"We were afraid we wouldn't be quick enough, and we'd get left behind." Her voice was almost musical but soft. And it affected me like a gentle stroke down my chest headed straight to my cock. I needed to squash that feeling hard. This girl wasn't up to taking me on, even if she'd wanted to.

I scrubbed a hand over my face. "I can't fuckin' believe this. Get your asses in the back seat and buckle up." I thought they'd get out the back, but both of them climbed over the back seat and did as instructed.

"Jesus, Roman, could you sound any more like a fuckin' old man?"

"Shut the fuck up, Brick." Then I muttered under my breath. "Motherfucker."

A couple miles down the road, Brick pulled the group over at a Buc-ee's and everyone in the club surrounded the Bronco as the women got out. And they were women, not older girls like I'd first thought. The shy one shrank behind her sister when the men crowded around them both. We didn't get into their personal space, but it was something that would have probably freaked any woman out.

"Jesus, guys, back off 'em!" Iris, Sting's ol' lady, was going to be a great match for our president. "Are you trying to frighten them to death?"

Sting chuckled, watching as his woman went to my stowaways. "Better do what she says, boys. She's a force of nature when she wants to be."

Naturally, we didn't need Sting's OK to back off. The girls looked terrified. The braver one had a determined look on her face as she lifted her chin. "We're not fragile. There're a lot of you. And you're all big."

"Of course, you're not fragile." Iris took her hand and reached for the other one. "Everyone, this is Winter. Her sister here is Serelda."

"You know them well, baby?" Sting stood close to his woman, but not close enough to spook the other two.

"No. But I'm looking forward to getting to know them." She gave Sting a pointed look. "Why don't we go take a quick break, then get something to eat for the road."

"Sounds like a plan. Cyrus. Eagle. Top off the tanks, then get any business done you need to. Once the ladies are good, we'll head on home."

I nodded at Sting before following the women. We kept a respectable distance, but stayed close enough to keep everyone away if we needed to. It didn't take them long in the bathroom, then all three of them headed to the food area. That took a little longer. It looked like Winter tried to coax her sister into getting something, but the other woman shook her head, refusing everything she offered.

"You notice the thin scars on 'em?" Brick stood beside me, watching the women with his hawklike gaze.

"Yeah. Noticed. Even on their faces."

"They got a story. We need that if they're gonna stay."

I turned my head. "They gonna stay?"

Brick shrugged. "Looks that way. Heard Sting talkin' to El Diablo. Black Reign prez wasn't surprised. Said Shotgun found where they snuck into your vehicle on their surveillance. El Diablo knows they're with us of their own free will, so he's willing to let things play out."

"Any idea what they're up to?"

"Not a clue. But before anyone gets any bright ideas, them girls ain't no spies."

That thought hadn't occurred to me. It should have. "You're sure about that? Wouldn't put it past Black Reign to try to put a plant in our club."

"I'm sure." Brick glanced at me, then headed to the women. He snagged a pack of Beaver Nuggets and handed them to Serelda. She took the bag and looked up at him but didn't say anything. He continued to stare at her until she nodded, and they all headed to the checkout.

I followed, wondering at the exchange between

the VP and Serelda. The sisters might be twins, but I'd already picked out a few differences between the two. Not only mannerisms, either. The pattern of scarring was different as well. Serelda had far more on her face than Winter. I hoped Black Reign had disposed of whomever did this to those girls, or I was going to have to ask our president for permission to go hunting.

As I followed them, Winter looked back over her shoulder at me. Her lips parted, and her delicate skin flushed a becoming shade of pink before she turned back around and walked faster toward the checkout. I found myself smiling despite my dark thoughts. I'd bet my last dollar that girl was attracted to me but too scared to flirt. It was just as well. Though she wasn't as young as Iris, she was still far younger than me. And obviously traumatized. The very last thing I wanted or needed was someone to babysit.

Even if that someone was the loveliest, most haunted creature I'd ever seen.

* * *

Winter

From the second the group from Iron Tzars rolled in, I knew this was what we'd been waiting for. They were the same as Black Reign in many respects, but for one very important fact. They had no idea what had happened to me and Serelda. There was no hiding the scars on the outside, but I'd hoped to at least try to conceal the ones on the inside. I didn't think Serelda could, but she was trying. Of the two of us, she'd suffered the most. Because she tried to protect me.

Then I'd found Roman. He was a complete mystery. One I wanted to find out about. He was protective of his brothers and Iris. She'd taken up with the president of Iron Tzars, and he seemed to be good for her. Before they were even an official couple, he'd done his best to protect her. Not always so she knew about it, but he'd had a goal in mind. Winning her trust. He'd called in his club, and they'd hunted down the trafficking ring that had taken Iris's sister and had brought her back. The tenacity and cunning they'd displayed in that one rescue mission told me this was where we needed to make our new home. The events leading up to us being in the middle of Six Flags over Truck Stop -- also known as Buc-ees -- loading up on enough junk food to feed an army, convinced me I'd made the right choice for Serelda and me.

Iris went with us to the bathroom and stayed outside the doors of our stalls, standing watch. Outside the bathroom, the guys stood watch. Once we'd finished, they all formed a protective ring around us as Iris encouraged us to get food. Serelda was too nervous to be interested in much, though I'd tried to coax her with foods I knew she'd like. It had all been for naught until the big guy they all called Brick handed her a bag of sweet, puffed nuggets.

At first, I didn't think she'd take the bag, but she had. Brick had been gentle but insistent. Once she agreed to take them, he left us, heading to the checkout to wait patiently. Serelda had ducked into my side, and I'd put an arm around her. She was trembling, but I thought it was more from surprise than fear. I'd noticed her looking at Brick from the moment he'd entered the Black Reign compound. He was older, but built like, well, a brick wall. Solid. Strong. Tall.

Though I liked the possibility of him being Serelda's protector, I still had no idea if he was the one for her. And I had my own problems to worry about. Because Roman had his eyes fixed on me since the moment I'd revealed our presence in his vehicle. I had no idea if it was distrust or interest he eyed me with, and I wasn't certain I wanted to find out. One thing was for sure, though. I was drawn to him. To me, he felt safe. Appearances could be deceiving. If I'd misjudged him or his club, we could be headed into trouble.

Brick took care of the bill, and we walked back to the vehicle, which was parked in the middle of several motorcycles now. Two of the club members leaned lazily against the truck, but I could see they were alert and very aware of their surroundings. One more mark in the club's favor. They took security seriously. Even in the middle of a place that was family friendly as they come.

"In you go." Roman startled me as he came up behind me and Serelda. I gasped in a breath and met his gaze. His eyes were black as night, though his hair was lighter and liberally dusted with gray. Short and shaggy, his beard had silver at the sides and chin. Though much of it was still dark, he was mostly a salt-and-pepper mix. One I found comforting to look at. He wasn't my age, though I was no young woman like Iris. I was thirty-five. Roman was probably pushing fifty. I'd thought it might freak me out since Serelda and I had been traumatized by older men, but it didn't. And Roman might be close in age to those men, but he was nothing like them in appearance or manner.

We complied, getting into the back seat. I helped Serelda with her seatbelt, then fastened my own. She was arguably the stronger of the two of us, but in some ways she was also the most fragile. She'd gone through so much. I'd vowed to protect her as viciously as she'd protected me. That included letting her retreat behind me from time to time. Now, she sat beside me. I had my arm around her, and she'd buried her face in my chest while she clung to me, trembling from the stress of being around so many unfamiliar people.

"You good?" Roman turned to regard us as he got in and shut the door. When I nodded, he started the vehicle. "Good. We'll be home in another hour and a half. Ain't as fancy as Black Reign's setup, but it's home. We'll make sure you've got a place to yourself so you can have some privacy but still be in the middle of our protection."

"Thank you." My voice was soft. While I was intrigued with Roman, I was also intimidated by him. "We appreciate you letting us continue on with you."

"Didn't have much choice, sweetheart. Couldn't very well leave you on the side of the road."

"No. I guess not." It was a shit thing to do to this club, but Rycks would never have allowed us to leave. Not because he held us prisoner. Because he tried his best to protect us. He had been since he and El Segador had rescued us in Las Vegas. Which was part of the problem. Sometimes, it felt like we were being smothered by the protection of Black Reign.

Leaving like we had had been a drastic move on our part. This club was an unknown. It was a stupid move, but my gut told me this was the right thing to do if we wanted a fresh start. After discussing it over several weeks with Serelda, we knew this was what we had to do.

"Gonna ask you one more time. Just us in here. I need to know. Did anyone from Black Reign hurt you? Are you runnin' 'cause you're afraid of someone there?"

I shook my head. "No! They've been nothing but good to us. All of them." I met his gaze in the rearview mirror before ducking my head. "It's... They protect us too much sometimes. We've been there a very long time. While we needed to be there for the most part, it's just time."

We were silent for a long time. Serelda still had her head against my chest. Occasionally I'd meet Roman's eyes in the mirror, but I couldn't hold them.

"You didn't think anyone in Black Reign would ever see you as anything but victims." It wasn't a statement. "Why not go to Salvation's Bane? Or Bones? Y'all are sister clubs. Right?"

"Same reason." I spoke softly, not really wanting to have this discussion in the car, but I knew he'd demand his answers one way or the other. Best to give in and get it over with. "Our stepsister is married to a man from Bones, and they know us at Salvation's Bane, too. They might not know everything, but they know enough."

"You know you can't keep this a secret. If you're gonna live alongside us, we have to know what your likely triggers are, and if there is anyone who might come lookin' for you."

"There's no one to come for us."

"Oh? El Diablo took care of your attackers?"

I shrugged. "No clue. At least, not the men who actually scarred us. There were more than one on multiple occasions. But the man who allowed it to happen, who facilitated it all and sold us out? Yeah. He's dead."

"You sure about that? We need to know so we can prepare for it."

"I know he's dead because I killed him." I stuck my chin up, finally meeting his gaze and holding it. There weren't many things in my life I was proud of, but this was one of them. Our father had sold us out. Allowed us to be raped and used in unspeakable ways. I hadn't been able to do it by myself, but I'd struck the killing blow and had reveled in it.

Roman raised an eyebrow. "You?"

"You don't think I could?" I dared him to say I couldn't.

He shrugged. "Don't know you that well, girl, but you don't look like the type."

"What type would that be?"

"The killin' type."

"Well, I did. Ask El Diablo or Rycks if you don't believe me. I cut that bastard like they cut me, then I stabbed him in the neck."

"I see."

"They were interrogating him and our stepmom. Cain was. At Bones. But I hid a knife and brought it with me when they let us tell our story. I cut him. Then stabbed him. He might have been tied up, but I still did it myself."

He grunted, taking his gaze from the mirror and continuing on. I had no idea what was going through his mind, but I wasn't about to gloss over that part of my life. It might have been years ago, but I got the only revenge I could. That part of my life still haunted me, but I refused to let it master me. It was why Serelda and I were here. To take back our lives in a place where no one had any preconceived notions about what we were able to handle. There was no way to conceal our past, but we could control the narrative. No one got to see how broken we were. We were strong.

Well, I was. Serelda tried, but she'd been withdrawn most of her adult life. Sometimes she came out of her shell, but it never lasted long. And she was never able to form attachments other than me. I hoped a complete change of scenery would give her the strength she needed to reinvent herself. If not, I'd call Lyric or Darcy and have Rycks come get us. Darcy was our stepsister and was married to a guy at Bones MC. We'd formed a bond of sorts over the years. Though Bones was still several hours away, it was far closer than Black Reign. Lyric was Rycks's woman. If we called both women, Darcy could get us away quickly and provide a safe place until Rycks came for us. At least, that was the plan.

"How old're you, girl?"

"I'm not a girl." I tried to put all the bravado and fierceness I could into my declaration. The last thing I wanted this man -- or his club -- to see was me and Serelda as two weak girls in need of protection. We weren't damsels in distress. Not anymore. "I'm thirty-five."

"How long you been at Black Reign?"

"Thirteen years."

"You go there after?" He didn't specify after what.

"Yes. El Segador and Rycks brought us back. It was the only place we felt safe."

"Why now?"

"Why what now?" I played dumb. Talking about this was more difficult than I'd thought, but I knew change would have to happen. At least, it was if we wanted to give this a shot.

He gave me an irritated look, and I sighed. "Look. It was just time. OK? We had time to study you while your club was there helping find Iris's sister. We decided this was the best chance we'd ever have to leave."

"You sayin' you didn't like it at Black Reign?"

"Not at all." I shook my head. "They were wonderful. They took us in when they didn't have to, but it's past time for us to get on with our lives. After watching all of you, we decided you were like Black

Reign. And Bones. And Salvation's Bane. You might skirt the law from time to time, but you're good people. We want a chance to live a life without people pitying us."

"I see your scars." He looked in the rearview mirror again. "Your sister seems to have more on her face than you do." He sounded matter-of-fact. He could have been discussing the weather for all the emotion he put into his observations. "I take it she took the brunt of the abuse?"

"She tried to protect me." It was all he was getting, so I hoped he would drop it.

"We protected each other." Serelda spoke softly, but she raised her head to meet Roman's gaze in the mirror. "It was how we survived."

"Who sold you out, Winter?" I knew that question was coming. It had been so long, and I tried not to think about it. I'd known going into this we'd have to relive our past to some degree. Didn't make it any easier.

"Our father."

Serelda whimpered and buried her face in my neck as I held her. Roman didn't question us any further. His grip on the steering wheel tightened until his knuckles were white. I noticed his jaw clenching and unclenching. He was angry. Logically, I knew he wasn't angry at us, just at the situation. It still hurt.

"We were victims," I continued. "But I got our revenge. Maybe we should have tried to get on with our lives sooner. I don't know. All I know is, this felt like the time to move on. So we did. I'm sorry we got you in the middle of our drama. If you don't want to take us on or if the condition of our staying involves… things we're not prepared to endure, we'll work out a way back to Florida. Or, at least, to Kentucky."

"Girl, don't piss me the fuck off." His growl *did* sound thoroughly pissed. "Ain't no woman at Iron Tzars doin' shit she don't want to. We'll make you a place to stay comfortably until you're ready to move on or you find your place in our club. Ain't no one gonna throw you out just 'cause you don't wanna be a club whore."

Again, Serelda whimpered and clutched my shirt tighter. I squeezed her tighter as I responded. "I'll make it known now. We don't want to be club whores. We're willing to work, but nothing sexual."

"We'll worry about that later. First thing when we get to the compound is to get you settled. Then there'll have to be a meeting. We'll have to discuss what to do. You know that, right?"

"We understand."

The rest of the drive was spent in silence. Thankfully, it wasn't long before we pulled through the chain-link gate and down a gravel road. The place seemed to have more land than Black Reign. It was ten minutes or so before we topped a rise to find a small community of buildings. Roman pulled up to the biggest and stopped the vehicle. Around us, the motorcycles parked one by one until everyone was off, clapping each other on the back and stretching sore muscles.

Roman opened the door on my side and helped us out. Serelda didn't look at anyone. She clung to my hand and looked down at her feet.

"She gonna be OK?" Roman spoke softly, his voice a rumbling vibration to my insides. I shivered. Despite the cold, I wasn't chilled. No. But for some stupid reason, I was insanely attracted to this guy.

"Yeah. We both need time to adjust, is all." I clutched Serelda's hand, giving it a tight squeeze to encourage her. "Once we get used to everyone, we'll both be good." I deliberately included myself in with Serelda, so she didn't feel stupid. Or weak.

"Might shoulda thought 'a that afore you left, little girl." His drawl sounded equal parts irritated and condescending. Which pissed me the fuck off.

Brick moved in front of us and held out his hand to Serelda. "Come with me, Tinkerbell. I'll get you settled while your sister castrates our enforcer over there."

Surprisingly, that got a giggle from Serelda. She looked up at me, a question in her eyes. I nodded. I wasn't sure why Brick was taking an interest in my sister, but she didn't seem to mind. The mere fact she was even considering going with the older, very big man was surprising but also a sign she felt safe with him. Anything that made Serelda feel safe was something she absolutely would get no matter what.

"Go if you want to, sissy," I said. "I'll be along in a bit."

Serelda didn't say anything, just nodded and followed Brick. She took the hand he'd held out and walked with him through the door of the clubhouse? It wasn't as big or fancy as Black Reign's, or even Salvation's Bane's. The latter had a converted firehouse they'd built onto. This was simpler. While the grounds and the main house were clean, there were signs of age. Made me wonder what the inside looked like.

I took in a deep breath before turning to face Roman. "You don't get to belittle my sister. You can try to talk down to me or make me feel like I've made a poor life choice, but I promise it won't work out well for you. You speak that way around Serelda again, and Brick is absolutely right about what will happen to you."

Roman didn't chuckle or blow me off like he was only joking or I took him the wrong way. Instead, he raised his chin in acknowledgment. "I apologize for my tone. Doesn't mean I'm wrong. Why would you leave your safe place? Especially if she's not comfortable with it?"

"It was time."

"Yeah, you said that." He crossed his arms over his chest. The man wore a Henley to perfection. It looked like it might be a couple sizes too small and like his arms and chest were ready to Hulk out of the thing any minute. I hated that I appreciated the view when the guy was obviously an asshole. "Still doesn't explain your motives. What do you hope to accomplish here?"

"We want to have a life outside of the bubble everyone's put us in. Is that so hard to imagine? While I love everyone at Bane and Reign, they're severely overprotective. Some of them saw the condition we were in when El Diablo rescued us and can't get past it. Because they can't get past it, it makes it harder for us to get past it. They don't even let the club girls anywhere near us for fear some of them will say something upsetting. I mean, they still do, sometimes, but we need to fend for ourselves. To function in society without being put in bubble wrap and being protected from harsh language."

"You *and* Serelda need this? Or you do?"

I opened my mouth to tell him to go to hell, then snapped it shut. Fuck, the man asked hard questions! "We both do," I said decisively. "She would never take this step on her own. But yes. I need it and acknowledge it while she would never. She'd stay in the background and be sheltered for the rest of her life. If she does, that means that motherfucker beat her. And I'll *never* allow that."

Roman held my gaze for long, long moments. It was like he was trying to figure me out. Like I was a science experiment he didn't know how to go about performing.

"You sure this is the best idea?" I opened my mouth to give him a piece of my mind again when he held up a hand. "Ain't criticizin' you. Just asking a question. Are you sure she's ready?"

"It's been more than a decade, Roman. If she's not ready now, she'll never be."

I turned away from him and followed Serelda and Brick into the clubhouse. This was truly a baptism by fire. If this club was anything like the clubs we'd been around before, the inside would be one big orgy in the main room this time of evening. I hoped it didn't give Serelda nightmares.

I hoped it didn't give *me* nightmares.

Chapter Two
Roman

This was fucking insane. No way these women were ready for this. Even if they'd been part of the club life for years, it was obvious they had more than a few issues. Serelda more than Winter, but I suspected Winter held hers inside better than her sister. It wasn't the parties and the sex going on at the parties and shit. I suspected they would struggle being around strange men in general. I needed to have a word with Sting if they were staying.

The party going on wasn't as wild as it normally was, but there were still more women undressed than dressed. Thus far, the only man who'd taken an ol' lady was Sting. This would be Iris's first time at a Tzars' party, and we were all anxious to see how she dealt with it.

I found Sting and Iris sitting at Sting's usual table with Iris sitting sideways in his lap. He had his arms around her securely as he talked to the other men at the table. I had no idea where Jerrica, Iris's sister, was, but suspected she'd passed out on the way up here and was in bed asleep. Likely, Sting had someone outside her door to let him and Iris know if she woke and needed them.

"Roman!" Sting lifted a hand to me, beckoning me to join them. "Fill me in on what's going on from your end."

I shrugged as I toed a chair around and straddled it, bracing my arms on the back. "Winter says they're looking for a fresh start. One where no one knows their story." I shook my head. "Not a good idea. Serelda seems like she's so fragile she'll break at the first cross word. Winter isn't really much better, though she hides it well."

"Well, I got the story from Rycks on the way up here. Ain't pretty. Even he doesn't know all of it, though. He's sure there's more, and the girls had it harder than they let on, but they've never told anyone at the club. And they've been there more than a decade." Sting rubbed a hand up and down his woman's arm like he was soothing her. I thought he might be soothing himself.

"They don't want to be coddled and wrapped in bubble wrap, but I'm not so sure they don't need it."

"They ain't girls, you know." Brick pushed his way through a group of club whores to get to the table. Big as he was, the man was always popular with the whores. When a couple of them would have followed him, Sting gave them hard, scathing looks, and they backed off. Brick ignored them completely. "They're in their thirties. I say they know their own minds. They get overwhelmed, it's up to them to say so."

"You've got no idea what they went though, Brick." Sting shook his head. "Ain't sure they belong here. Hell, ain't sure how they survived at Black Reign. They need to be in a little house with a fuckin' white picket fence protected by a loving husband who dotes on their every move."

"I think you're not giving them enough credit." It surprised me that Iris spoke up. It wasn't a formal meeting in Church, but Iris was new to everything here, including life in an active MC. Every now and then, I'd see her looking around the room, wide-eyed and somewhat in shock herself. If anyone questioned whether or not she was going to be a good ol' lady to our president, now was the moment of truth. "They survived hell. They can survive here."

Sting gave her a look of pride before schooling

his features once again. "Let's give it time. Deal with any issues as they happen. In the meantime, treat them like you would any other woman here who's not a club whore."

"Pres, there ain't no women here who ain't club whores." That was Cyrus. Regardless of his statement, he wasn't stupid. He had trouble relating to other people's feelings and thought everyone should just do what he said, but he wasn't a bad guy.

"Except me." Iris said, her face a hard mask of anger. "Treat them with the respect you better treat me with."

Brick barked out a laugh before smothering it with a cough.

Cyrus blinked and shook his head. "This is one of those times I sound like a dumbass. Isn't it?"

Brick clapped him on the shoulder. "Wish I could say otherwise, man, but yeah. It's one of those things to do with feeling. You'll figure it out eventually. Just try not to be too big of a bastard as you do."

"Where are the kids? Everyone asleep?"

"Yes." Iris smiled a contented, happy smile. "Jerrica is sharing a room with Monica, Daisy, and Clover. Clover still isn't talking, but then she hasn't since she came to the home. But she smiled when she saw the bed Sting helped me fix for her."

"You can do wonders for a girl child with a pink comforter and fairy lights." Sting beamed, looking for all the world like a proud papa.

"Fuck, Sting." Smoke shook his head as he took a swig of his beer. "Not a daddy a month yet and already those girls stole your man card. Your woman gonna keep it or she gonna let you have it back when we go on rides?"

Sting just rolled his eyes. "Keep it up, and you'll

have guard duty from now till next Christmas."

That got everyone laughing. Normally this would be when I'd find me a woman for the night. Relax and fuck until I was tired. I didn't want to tonight. My head wasn't in it. Instead, I went to the area we'd set up for guests at the very back of the main clubhouse. I figured that was where Brick had put Winter and Serelda. At least until we had time to relocate them to one of the houses in the compound.

I walked down the hall and saw Winter's pale blonde locks disappearing through a door at the end of the hallway. When I got to the door, I knocked lightly. There was some shuffling before the door opened. Winter stood in the doorway, blocking my view and holding the line that protected her sister from prying eyes.

"Just thought I'd check on you." It was lame, but it didn't feel right not going to her. And it was definitely Winter I had a pull toward.

"We're fine. Thanks for asking." She stared at my chest, not meeting my gaze.

"You should come down to the party. Meet some of the guys. Iris is there with Sting. Stick with her, and the club whores'll stay outa your way."

"I suppose we should." She didn't seem convinced, looking over her shoulder. Probably to get Serelda's opinion, though I couldn't see the other woman. Winter guarded her sister like a pitbull. That was easy to see.

"There'll be food. Always is. I'll be happy to take you down."

Again, she looked over her shoulder. "Maybe I'll bring Serelda something back."

"We can do that."

"Go with him, Winter." The sound coming from

the inside of the room was eerily similar to Winter's but husky. As if she didn't use her voice much. "I'm tired from the trip. I'll just take a bath, then rest."

"I'll bring you back something. You need to eat." Winter was close to tears. I could see it on her face. Was she rethinking their decision to leave their home?

"You know, I can arrange for you to go back to Black Reign if you want. You're welcome to stay, but don't think you have to just because you're already here." I tried to sound gentle when I wanted to make the decision for her. Anyone could tell Serelda wasn't ready, and Winter wasn't being separated from Serelda.

"No." She put her shoulders back and finally met my gaze. Her features hardened, and she put her chin up. "We're fine. We just need some time to adjust."

"She can take as much time as she needs. You too. No one's gonna pounce on either of you. Take some time to get to know us -- but do it in your own time."

"Wow. Seems like you might have made your peace with us being here."

"Honey, ain't got no problem with you bein' here. I know you have emotional scars, and those are the toughest to heal. Some people never do."

"Scars don't heal. They always leave a mark." She tugged self-consciously at her sleeves. They were long, but she'd pulled them up her forearms out of her way. Several scars from what looked like thin cuts crisscrossed her skin everywhere I could see. Now she covered her arms as low as the shirt would rest on her wrists. It made me wonder if she was covered in those scars all over her body. My guess was yes. Made me want to claw a motherfucker's heart out.

"But you're tougher for them. You survived. You

endured. You went on."

She stepped outside and shut the door behind her. "No. We didn't. At least we didn't get on with our lives. Not really."

"This is what you meant before. About starting over."

"It's what we both need, but Serelda even more than me. We both need a fresh start. I'm hoping we can find it here. We only have to be brave enough to take it."

The look on her face, the fierce pride in her voice made me believe Winter could take whatever she wanted. She was slight of build and delicate-looking, but inside she had a stout heart. Just made me that much more interested in her.

Winter headed down the hallway ahead of me and marched straight to the common room where the party was in full swing. Instead of hunting down Iris like I thought she might do, she went to the bar and signaled the prospect. He placed a bottle of beer in front of her before popping the top. She took a long pull while she looked around the room, sizing the place up. I leaned against a nearby wall watching her. I wanted to see what she'd do. How she'd react if approached by one of the brothers. Would she flinch back? Tell him to take a hike?

Retreat back to her room?

I didn't like the thought of her being scared of any of us. Made me want to warn everyone off. The girl had obviously been through enough. She didn't need a bunch of horny bikers making passes at her.

She finished her beer, then signaled for another.

"Word is you got a sister, little lady. She not with you?" The prospect leaned one elbow against the bar and gave her a cocky grin.

"She's resting. It was a long trip." Winter didn't smile at the younger man. The prospect -- Deacon -- wasn't deterred. He got himself a beer and opened the top, then clinked the neck with hers.

"Glad you ventured out. I was hoping I'd get to meet you."

Winter turned her full attention to him then. "You were? Why?" She didn't make it sound like a question. More like a demand. Like she sensed a trap and was determined not to fall for it.

Deacon shrugged. "I always enjoy meeting beautiful women."

"Looks like there's plenty of women here for you without me or my sister being on your radar." Her face hardened. "Stay away from my sister."

Deacon raised his hands in surrender. "Hey. I'm not interested in hurtin' anyone. I just like havin' a good time. Someone don't wanna party with me, I won't be forcin' 'em." The only reason Deacon got to live was his tone of voice and his expression. He didn't laugh her off, and he wasn't making fun of her or her fears. "Just wantin' the two of you to feel welcome."

"Uh-huh." Winter eyed him as she took another pull from her beer. "I don't see you trying to make Iris feel welcome."

"That's cause Iris is our prez's ol' lady. You don't mess with a brother's woman. I'm nice to her. I respect her. I'll protect her the same as I'd protect our president. But I ain't gonna get cozy with her."

"And you were trying to get cozy with me?" Winter scowled at him.

He gave her a charming smile that had me wanting to beat him to a bloody pulp. I had to force myself to stand there and listen to the son of a bitch and not act on my instincts.

"Honey, any man in this club who don't wanna get cozy with you is a Goddamn fool. You'd make a fierce ol' lady."

"You don't know me," she snapped, looking angry as hell. "If this is some kind of bet where you try to get in my pants so your brothers can laugh at me when I make it easy for you, you're wasting your time. I have no interest in sex with anyone here." She snatched her beer. "Excuse me."

"That's not what this is," Deacon called after her as she stood to leave.

Winter moved to the other side of the room, where she stood by herself and continued to try to read the room. She was close to a group of club girls, and I knew there would be a confrontation soon. The only question was how many fireworks would be set off.

I kept my eye on her but moved to the bar where Deacon shook his head as he stared at her. "That woman's a biker's wet dream." He was talking to himself more than me, but I felt the need to respond.

"She is. I'd suggest you treat her like you would Iris, though. Her man might get the idea you're encroaching on his territory."

Deacon didn't take his eyes off Winter. "Oh? Who's her man?" I doubt the pup even knew who he was talking to.

"Me, you dumb shit."

He whipped his head around in surprise, his mouth open. "Roman? I'm sorry, man. Didn't know you'd claimed her."

"Ain't yet. 'Cause she just got here. You pass the word around. Anyone thinkin'a movin' in on her, better be ready to tangle with me."

"I'll spread the word." The other man nodded gravely, taking everything I said seriously. Because of that, I decided to not give him a beat down. For now.

I watched as a club whore approached Winter, looking her up and down. Jezlynn said something that made Winter's face harden. She didn't back down from the other woman but didn't respond to her either. Just gave her a steady gaze. When Jezlynn continued, the other women laughed and spoke amongst themselves, obviously supporting Jezlynn in whatever mischief she was causing. I saw the exact moment when whatever they said to Winter hit their mark.

"Ah, hell…" Deacon saw it too.

"Yeah. I think you're right."

* * *

Winter

"Bet it hurts to look in the mirror, don't it, honey? I know a good cosmetologist who could probably do something with your face." The bitch didn't sound like she cared one way or the other. I knew she was just trying to hurt me. She succeeded. I'd known this would happen. It was the only reason I was out there now instead of helping Serelda get settled. I wanted to get the women in the club used to seeing my scars so maybe when Serelda joined me away from our room they'd leave her alone for the most part. Instead of rising to the bait, I just looked at the woman and let her and her friends continue.

"That why you wear long sleeves and those hideous pants? You got 'em all over you?" That came from one of the women behind the first one. A gaggle of club whores. Lovely.

"No competition there," another of the women commented. "No biker around here'd want a used-up whore."

"Yeah," the first one continued. "Bet whoever

put those scars on you got tired of your bitchin' and whinin'. You know, if you'd learn how to suck cock and fuck a man properly, he won't cut you." They all laughed.

The image of the men who'd cut me flashed through my mind. Laughing at Serelda and me. Humiliating us. *All the blood making them slide over me while they…*

NO!

I was not that powerless girl any longer. I'd fought back. I'd killed my father for selling us as whores to those men and others before them the first chance I got. The only reason I hadn't killed the men he'd sold us to was because I had no idea who they were or how to find them. But these bitches? Yeah. I could deal with them. I'd make them pay for their callous words and, hopefully, make them think twice about saying anything like that again. Especially where Serelda could hear.

Before I even realized I was going to do it, I smashed the bottle of beer I'd been nursing on the edge of the table, breaking it off into a jagged piece. I held it by the neck, the broken bottle now a deadly weapon. It wasn't as good as the knife I'd had the day I'd killed my father, but it would be enough.

I lunged forward, swinging the bottle at the first woman. I caught her cheek with the glass edge and she screamed, slapping her hand over the cut. It wasn't shallow. I'd laid her cheek open enough there was no way it wouldn't leave a horrible scar. I should know. I'd had it done to me enough. The sight nearly made me vomit. It took so much effort to just remain standing I wasn't sure how long I could manage to stay on my feet and keep from puking. But I couldn't let it show. So I raised my chin and continued as I wanted my relationship with all the club whores here to proceed.

"Now you can look at yourself in the mirror. Maybe if you'd learned how to suck my pussy with that mouth instead of running it, you wouldn't have gotten cut." My voice was calm and steady when I was trembling with rage inside.

Surprisingly, none of the men interfered. They'd stopped to watch, and more than one snickered at my comment, but they didn't try to talk either of us down. All but one of the girls with the leader backed off. She grabbed her own bottle and broke it like I had, a maniacal gleam in her eyes.

"You wanna fight, bitch? Then come on!"

She shoved the first woman out of the way and charged me with a battle cry. I side-stepped her and swung the bottle in my hand in a sweeping arch, catching the back of her shoulder in a deep slice. All those self-defense classes Rycks had made us take were finally paying off. She cried out and whipped around.

"You fuckin' cunt!"

"There's more where that came from." I beckoned her to me. "Come get some more."

She did, running at me again in the same way. Again, I spun out of her way. This time, I stabbed her side as my momentum carried me around. I knew I'd gotten close to her kidney. She was slender, so it was entirely possible I'd hit my target even though I hadn't hit her from the back. She screamed, clamping a hand to her injury. Blood poured between her fingers. Nausea bubbled, and I knew if I focused too long on the blood I'd be sick and any respect I'd just won would evaporate. Only then did any of the men make a move toward us.

"That's enough." Brick's order wasn't one

anyone could ignore. It was barked with the authority of someone who could and would make your life a living hell if you dared to disobey him. "Eagle, take Jezlynn to the infirmary. Stitches can't patch her up, get him to call in a favor. But she stays here. No hospitals."

"If Stitches can't fix this she could die!" That was from the first woman. The other one I'd cut.

"Shoulda thought about that before gettin' in a bar fight with more than your fists. She goes to the hospital, they ask questions. Ain't puttin' the club in danger cause'a her stupidity."

"You gonna punish that bitch? You allowing some outsider to come in here and disrespect us now?"

"Jezlynn," Brick said, leveling his gaze on the women. "You're about two seconds from gettin' kicked out. And you know what that means." For some reason the other woman paled. She shook her head and backed off. "We gonna have a problem?"

"No, Brick. No problem." Though her tone was subdued and subservient, she threw me a venomous look before turning to leave. Someone had given her a napkin to put over her cheek, but blood had already soaked through.

Slippery, sticky, fluid over my body while the men wrapped their arms around me to hold me still. Taking their pleasure. Making me lick my own blood from their fingers…

I'd reached my limit with the blood. If I didn't leave now, I was going to be sick.

Knowing I needed a distraction and that there was no way they'd just let me leave the common room, I decided I'd better start with Brick before he started with me. I gripped the neck of my broken bottle tighter. "I ain't sorry for what I done. Jezlynn asked for it, and the other one tried to cut me first."

"No one's takin' you to task, Winter." He shook his head before reaching out a hand palm up, obviously wanting my weapon.

"You'll pardon me if I don't give up my only defense." I made no move to surrender the broken bottle.

He nodded. "OK. Fair enough. Probably shoulda stopped that before it escalated. The whores are territorial. They see you as a threat, whether you are or not."

"My suggestion would be to let them know me and my sister aren't interested in encroaching on their territory. I know the score. I knew moving to a club we didn't know would involve risks exactly like this one. Though, I confess, I never thought I'd have to injure someone that badly."

"What did she say to you?"

Surprisingly, it was Roman, stalking toward us, who asked the question. There was an odd look on his face. A cross between fury and... hunger? But why would he be looking at *me* like that?

"Nothing I should've reacted that badly to. She was looking to get under my skin, and she did."

Roman raised his voice so it carried over the whole room. "Maybe this lesson has been learned by everyone, so you don't have to repeat it."

Brick raised an eyebrow but didn't contradict Roman. "I heard what she said. You're right. Bitch deserved it." He raised his voice so the whole room could hear him. "If we're all finished here, I'd like to get back to the fuckin' party." The big man sounded irritated but had a look of satisfaction on his face. "You want to sit with Sting and Iris, Winter? They've got room at their table for you."

"That an order?" I put my chin up. It was the last

thing I wanted, but I didn't really expect anything else. I took several deep breaths, trying to calm my roiling stomach.

Roman rolled his eyes before taking my hand. "Yeah. It's a fuckin' order. Come on."

He led me to the table where Iris and Sting sat. Iris got to her feet with a huge smile on her face. Surprisingly, seeing the other woman helped me center myself.

Breathe in slowly. Out slowly. In. Out.

"I'm so glad you came down to join us!" She hugged me tightly before letting go. Iris was a stunning beauty. I hadn't seen her smile often while Black Reign searched for her sister, but now she was positively beaming. "Are you settling in?"

I blinked. "Is that it?"

"What?"

"You're not going to address the pink elephant in the room? I just stabbed someone!"

Iris shrugged. "Yeah. You did. If the guys ain't worried about it, I'm not. From the look of things, she had it coming."

"Well, when you put it like that." I knew then I was going to like Iris. The younger woman reminded me a lot of Jezebel, El Diablo's wife.

"I'm glad you're here, Winter. I hope Serelda feels comfortable enough to join us soon. We're all going to be great friends." Iris reached over and gripped my hand with a bright smile.

I had no doubt she was right. We'd be fast friends.

Chapter Three

Roman

If I lived to be a hundred, I'd never forget the sight of Winter as she took care of business with the club girls. The look on her face was fierce and determined. And the viciousness with which she delivered her punishment to Jezlynn gave me the hard-on from hell.

I sat next to Winter as she and Iris chatted lightly. Sting had his arm around Iris, a smirk on his face as if he knew exactly what a lucky bastard he was to have Iris as his ol' lady. Before, I hadn't really seen the appeal. To me, women had been a pleasant pastime, but I'd never really connected with one on an emotional level. Maybe I'd just never cared. But this girl… Yeah. I knew her past. Knew how she viewed it as shaping her present. By God, I wanted to be the one to claim her future.

Glancing at Sting, I could tell he knew something was up with me. He didn't call me out on it or say anything, but he gave me a knowing look. Yeah. I was going through a struggle similar to the one he went through with his woman. Did I keep her? My loyalties would be divided if I did. There was no way I could put my club over my woman. I wasn't built like that. I protected what was mine. So my club, or my woman? It was an impossible choice.

"I need to get back to Serelda." Winter stood to leave. "Thanks so much for taking time to get to know me. I hope we can find a place to fit in here. Having watched how the Iron Tzars men worked together to get Jerrica back, I know they're good people." Winter smiled warmly at Iris. "I'm so glad you found Sting, Iris. I'm glad you and your sister have a strong protector." Winter's sincere comment dropped a veil over her expression. Just like that, I could see shadows of her past haunting her. My heart went out to her, and everything inside me demanded I make life perfect for this woman. I wanted to find the men her father let touch her and strangle them with their own entrails.

"I'll walk you to your room." I stood and snagged Winter's hand before she could resist. I'd studied Winter and knew she wouldn't draw attention to herself by protesting. As long as I didn't do anything to make her uncomfortable or embarrass her, she'd go along with me to avoid an open confrontation. Jezlynn had pushed her too far, and that was the only reason she'd fought back. If I was right, one fight was all she was up for in a day. And only because the club girls had challenged her first.

Before I took her out of the common room, I snagged some burgers and chips to take up to Serelda. Winter gave a soft gasp as she looked at the plate.

"I forgot to get Serelda something." Her voice was barely above a whisper, and she looked horrified. "How could I have forgotten?"

"Relax, honey. This is all overwhelming. Besides, you *did* get in a bar fight and stab someone." I teased her gently, but that seemed to make her discomfort worse.

"I'm so sorry. I shouldn't have done that." She glanced over her shoulder. Probably to Sting and Iris's table.

"Yeah, you shoulda. No one gets to talk to you like that, Winter." My tone came out harsher than I meant it to, but it was the fucking truth. It made her focus on me, though. She turned back to face me, her eyes wide. "No one. Not me. Not Sting. Damned sure not a jealous club whore." I sighed, knowing I needed to tone it down. "Come on, babe. Let's get back to your room so Serelda has something to eat if she wants." She let me take her hand once more without protest.

I took her back through the clubhouse, until we stopped at her door. She looked up at me with those pale blue eyes of hers, and I was fucking lost. "Don't look at me like that, honey."

She blinked rapidly and looked away, only to glance at me again. I liked to think it was because she couldn't take her eyes off me, but she was probably making sure I didn't pounce on her like I probably looked ready to do.

"I don't understand. How am I looking at you?"

"Like you want me to claim you. Make you mine." She shook her head slightly, but her eyes widened, and her lips parted. "Yeah, baby. I think that's exactly what you want."

I took the plate, balancing it in one hand. With my free hand, I gripped the back of her neck and pulled her to me. Her hands landed on my chest. Instead of pushing me away, her fingers curled into my shirt and bunched the material in her fists. With a groan, I brought my mouth to hers, sweeping my tongue inside as she whispered, "Sweet Jesus…" like a plea. Maybe she was praying for deliverance. If she was, her actions belied her prayers. Because, God above, the woman kissed me back like she'd been waiting her whole life for this kiss. I wanted to howl with the rightness of it. I also knew without question Winter would be mine.

She was sweet. Like morning dew warmed by the first rays of sunlight. Her hunger mirrored my own, though she was tentative. The longer I kissed her, the more she let herself go. God, I wanted to see what she would be like once she unleashed the pent-up passion inside her! Winter was a powder keg waiting for the right man to make her explode. Though I hadn't been sure at first, I knew in my heart I was that man. *Her* man. She was still fragile and probably wasn't ready to take me on, but I could get her there. I was sure there were things I needed to know about her past, but I was a patient man when I wanted something badly enough. And I wanted Winter with every fiber of my being.

Very gently, I ended the kiss, wrapping my arm around her shoulders instead of gripping her nape to hold her steady. I pulled her to me and let her cling while we both caught our breath. I could feel her trembling, but she still clung to my shirt. One arm slid up my chest to hook around my neck, and I breathed a sigh of relief. She was accepting me. At least for the moment.

"You good, baby?"

She didn't speak, but nodded, still clinging to me. I kissed the top of her head before resting my chin there and held her for long moments. Finally, she pushed away and turned to open the door to her and Serelda's room.

"Thank you, Roman." She didn't look at me. "For everything."

"You have my number in your phone?"

She nodded.

"I want you to text me. Or call. If you need anything. If you want to talk."

She turned to look at me over her shoulder. "Do you really mean that?"

"I do, Winter. I expect it. I find out you needed something -- anything -- and didn't call me, I'll be pissed. You get lonely or wake up in the night and can't go back to sleep, I expect a call."

She glanced over my shoulder. "Are you going back to the party?"

I held her gaze. "I'll be there with Sting and Iris. Maybe Brick. No one else. You want to join me, you're always welcome."

Again, she looked over my shoulder before ducking her head. I glanced behind me where a club whore had draped herself lazily against the wall two doors down from us. It was obvious she was waiting on me to leave Winter so she could approach me. Yeah, it was going to take some time for the whores to get the message. I didn't blame them. It was what they were here for. To provide sex to the men. They were chosen specifically for that purpose. They kept the club members satisfied when they were called upon, and they entertained any guests we invited over. Especially if there was business involved. A little bit of playing always made for smoother deals. I'd taken my fill from time to time, but never again. It often made for competition amongst the women. Each of them had men they enjoyed or wanted for themselves. They never landed a brother for more than a night or two at a time, but it didn't prevent them from trying. Besides, Sting was the only one of us with a woman. Warlock had had Bev, but that was it. And they were both gone now. The whores hadn't adapted to the new surroundings yet. They would.

"Will you have… company?"

"No, Winter. The only woman I'll have with me is you. You don't feel like joining us now, that's OK."

Her lips parted on a little gasp. "I don't… I don't understand." Her voice was so soft it was hard to make out her words. Her face flushed scarlet, and she brought her fingertips to her lips, then moved her palm to cover the worst scar over her cheek, which she'd tried to cover with heavy makeup.

"Then I'll spell it out for you, baby." I stepped back into her space, placing one arm beside her head on the door. "I'm not gonna be with a club girl or any other woman for any reason. I got my eye on you. I'm not a nice man, but I never go back on my word, and I never betray those I care about. I won't betray you, Winter. Not with another woman. Not for any reason."

"You don't know me. I'm not even sure if I can..." She trailed off, swallowing nervously. "I have a past that's not pretty."

"We all have pasts, Winter. Yours might be uglier than some, but everyone has things that haunt them."

"But mine might not let me carry things any further than we just went."

"Then I'll have a lot of showers in my future to take things in hand." I leaned in and kissed her lips lightly. "You don't want to take a chance, that's your choice. But if you trust me, I swear I'll never betray that trust."

"You'll stop if I say?"

"Honey, always. No matter when or why. I will never hurt you. Especially not like that."

She nodded several times, still casting furtive glances at the club girl watching us intently. "I -- I'll think about it." With a glance up at me and a small smile, she took the plate back, entered her room and shut the door.

For the first time in my life, I felt a thrill of... something. Excitement? Nervousness? Peace... Seemed like an oxymoron, but there it was. I'd known I wanted her before, but this...

Winter was the woman I wanted for myself. She had scars. Both physical and emotional. She wouldn't be easy, but I knew in my very soul she would be worth all the effort it would take to be with her. Winter… was mine. She seemed to have destroyed her demons, but they still haunted her. Anyone could see that just by looking at her. Tonight, when I'd kissed her? I think that was the first time she'd ever considered she might want something from a man. I could see her struggling but wanting to embrace the pleasure she'd found. With gentleness and a lot of coaxing, I thought I could give her what she needed. And make her crave so much more. The tentative nature she showed to me now was so at odds with the women who'd taken it to the club girls harassing her that it was oddly stimulating. I didn't want a simpering female, and that wasn't Winter. But she *was* vulnerable. Which meant I had to be careful.

I rested my palm against the door after she'd closed it. So help me God, if it was the last thing I did, I'd make that woman realize she was so much more than the sum of her scars.

* * *

Winter

I'd never felt so alive as I did when Roman had kissed me. I stood there with my back to the door, the plate of food for Serelda in my hands, and my heart raced. I wanted to run back out that door and straight into his arms. At the same time, I was terrified.

"Winter?" Serelda came from the bedroom. "What's wrong? What happened?" Serelda looked alarmed and like she might dissolve into tears at any moment.

"Nothing. I'm fine. I swear." I put my hand over my chest. My breasts ached, and I was sure my nipples were poking hard against the material of the sports bra

I wore.

"You're not fine!" Serelda took the plate and practically tossed it to the table before locking the door and propping a chair against it. I wanted to reassure her, but I could barely catch my breath.

"Really, Serelda. It's good." It was all I could manage.

She snagged my hand and drew me farther into our suite of rooms, away from the door. "What happened? I'll call Rycks, and he'll send Viper and Cain after us."

"No! I swear, Serelda, everything is good." I pulled my sister into my arms and hugged her. "I'm fine."

"Tell me. Please. I don't want to stay here. I want to go back home." Tears did stream down Serelda's cheeks now. Her whole body trembled, and she was pale as a sheet.

"Sit down and I'll tell you. Come." I moved to the window seat where she'd set up a nest of blankets and pillows. She'd liked to sit next to the window in our room at Black Reign and watch the ocean or read a book. It didn't surprise me she'd claimed this place for herself.

I took her hands firmly in mine. "I kissed Roman. Well, he kissed me, but I kissed him back."

Serelda blinked several times, her mouth opening, then closing again. "You... what?"

"I know, right?" I giggled, unable to help myself. "I kissed Roman. He wants... well, he said he had his eye on me. He said he wasn't going to be with another woman. That he wanted me."

"You believe him?" Serelda tilted her head to the side. I could tell she wasn't sure what to think.

"I don't know! I want to." I sighed happily. I felt

like a schoolgirl with her first crush. In a way, I guess I was. Our father had whored us out in our early teens. Before I'd ever taken an interest in boys. After that? Well. It had taken me more than a decade to allow another man to touch me. I'd been attracted to Roman from the second I'd seen him. Now that I'd had a taste of what it would be like to let him have me, I thought I might be ready.

"Are you sure he won't hurt you? I don't really see it in any of these guys, but I don't want to be wrong."

"I don't think he'd hurt me. Not physically, at least. Though, I think it might break my heart if… Well, I can't imagine letting another man kiss me like he did. If he went to another woman… If I'm just a novelty to him…"

"Just be careful." Serelda leaned in and put her arms around me, hugging me to her. We often held each other when we were scared. It had started soon after the first time our father had given us to a man. He'd wanted to play with twins and had taken our virginity. It hadn't been pretty, and we'd both huddled in our closet for two days before our father had dragged us out to meet the second "client."

The second those memories shoved their way into my mind, I shuddered. All arousal I'd felt disappeared in a flash. Who was I kidding? There was no way I could be with Roman. Not in any meaningful physical way.

"I will, sis." I tried to put on some bravado even though I knew Serelda would see right through me.

"Don't let Dad win." Serelda's soft plea found its way into my head. The pain in her voice was enough to push my demons back behind the door I tried so hard to keep them behind, and I could breathe again. "Run with this if you trust him. I can always call Rycks. He'll get us out if we get into trouble."

"I know. I'll be all right. I'm just a little scared and overwhelmed. But I really want him, Serelda. For the first time in my life, I think I'm ready to try to be in a normal relationship."

She pulled back, swiping at her tears before brushing her thumb under my eye to catch my own. "You know you'll have to tell him. Right?"

"I don't want to." I turned to look out the window, knowing she was right. "He'll see me as a victim. Even after what happened today."

"Wait. What do you mean after what happened today? I thought you kissing Roman was what happened today."

I winced, turning back to face my sister with a sheepish grin. "I might have accidentally gotten into a fight."

"You what? But you hate violence!"

"I know!" I twisted my hands together, glancing up at Serelda before looking down again. "And I might have cut one of the club girls with a broken beer bottle."

"Winter!" When I looked at Serelda she was fighting a smile. The woman actually looked happy about this.

"Yeah, well. I also stabbed another club girl. But only after she tried to stab me." I hurried to finish, needing to get it out before Winter could say anything to make me *not* tell her all of it.

To my surprise, she did laugh then. "I don't know why that surprises me. I guess she pushed you just a little too far."

"Yeah. She did. I'll have to watch my back, though. She let it go now, but I'm sure that won't last long."

"Not if they're anything like the girls in the other clubs. Not unless Roman makes you his ol' lady."

"Slow down, sister. We're not nearly that far yet. We've only kissed once."

She laughed, hugging me once before getting up from her seat. "You have to start somewhere. Come on. I want to see what you brought to eat. You hungry?"

"Nah. You go on." I hadn't eaten, but I wasn't hungry. Too many butterflies in my stomach for that. "I think I'm going to take a shower and go to bed. It's been a long, tumultuous day."

"I'll save you something. You can reheat it later if you want." Serelda gave me a smile and gripped my shoulder.

"It's OK. Eat all you want. I'll get something fresh tomorrow. You want to think about going down with me?" I knew it was pushing, but I was beginning to believe we both needed pushing. I'd been pushed by the club girls. I could push Serelda in a gentler way.

She looked away. "I don't know. Maybe." She shrugged, her head down. "We'll see."

Having planted that seed in Serelda's mind for later, I went to the bathroom for a shower. As I undressed, I looked at myself in the mirror. I usually tried to avoid my reflection. It was a stark reminder of everything that had happened to me I'd tried so hard to forget. Scars crisscrossed my entire body. Even my face. The worst scars, though, were on the inside. Those scars were the ugliest of all.

I hung a towel over the mirror like Serelda and I usually did. Would I ever be able to look at myself in the mirror and not flinch? It had been more than a decade, and I still cringed every time I saw my reflection. I'd been a beautiful girl. The woman? Not so much.

As usual, I hurried through the shower, not wanting to touch myself any more than I had to. After all these years, the scars abrading my palms and the feel of the water slipping over me nauseated me. Using a washcloth or loofah didn't help either. It seemed like I could feel the raised skin through anything. It was the same reason I didn't put on lotion. I tried to stay out of the spray of water as much as I could, only stepping under it to rinse.

I didn't wash my hair because I just wanted to crawl into bed. I'd wash it in the sink tomorrow and deal with the long mass then. I'd have to because I wanted to wear it down to cover as many of the scars on my face I could. Makeup helped, but I had to cake it on thick. I use a silicone gel underneath and a thick foundation to smooth everything over. It was a horrid ritual that took time, but it was the only way to hide the nasty things. And I didn't want to see Roman unless my scars were covered.

Roman. God, the man was larger than life! He was quiet most of the time. No-nonsense. When he needed to take charge, he did so without hesitation. I saw the way the club girl had looked at him. She wanted him. What woman wouldn't? He was tall, muscled, powerful. Everything a girl needed to keep her safe. He was the type of man to defend what was his with everything in him. At least, I thought he was. He'd also seemed to have claimed me. I hoped I was right about that, because that was the way I wanted it to be.

I lay in bed for a long time. Just thinking. I replayed the fight in my head. Roman's response. The response of the other club members. Sting and Brick hadn't batted an eyelash until I'd stabbed that woman.

Then they hadn't come after me, but her. They'd made it sound like it was the club girl's fault. I'd attacked first, but I'd been provoked. They seemed to understand that.

I sighed, turning over to glance at the clock. One twenty-three. Had I dozed off or had I been thinking that long? I glanced at my phone on the dresser. It was way too late to call Roman. Besides, I was sure he was just being nice. Or trying to reassure me he wouldn't be with another woman. But why? Was it all an elaborate scheme to get me to have sex with him? Again, why? He could have any woman he wanted. I wasn't even sure I could have sex with anyone. He'd said it didn't matter, but I knew in my heart it did. What man as rugged and strong as Roman wouldn't need sex? And if I couldn't give it to him, he'd get it somewhere else. And I'd be heartbroken.

No. Roman wasn't the man for me. But I wanted him to be.

Chapter Four
Winter

I woke up with Serelda's back solidly against mine. We often slept like that because we felt safer. Even in the years since we'd been safe behind the walls of Black Reign, it was a habit we'd never broken.

"You going to the common room for breakfast?" Serelda looked over her shoulder as she spoke. I should have known she was awake. We always woke together, no matter how long either of us had been asleep.

"I thought I might. You want to come with me?"

She was silent for a long while. I thought she might have gone back to sleep, but she let out a defeated sigh, then answered me. "No. Not today. Will you bring me back something?"

"You know I will."

"You know what I like."

"I do."

I got up and showered, washing my hair thoroughly. The towel from the night before was still over the mirror. I didn't remove it until I'd brushed and dried my hair. Then, with a sigh, I removed it long enough to put the putty-like silicone on my face to smooth out the scars over my skin, then cover it all with a thick foundation. Years of this same ritual helped me to hurry. Before leaving the bathroom, I replaced the towel.

Serelda was still in bed and had gone back to sleep. The scars on her face were much worse than mine because she'd tried to protect me. That had been her punishment.

A rage built inside me. It always did when I remembered how she'd protected me from those vile men when I couldn't protect myself. I wanted to kill them all. Every single one. But I had no way of doing it. Not when I didn't know who they were. Our father was dead. So was our stepmother. They were the only two people I knew of who could tell us the names of the men they'd sold us to. Truthfully, there were so many I doubt either of them could have remembered anyway.

Taking a breath, I closed my eyes and pictured a quiet, sunny meadow. The only sounds around me were birds singing, summer bugs buzzing, and a warm breeze rustling the leaves of trees surrounding the meadow. I pictured that scene in my mind until I could almost feel the wind on my face.

Deep breath in. Let it out slowly. Repeat.

Once I was steady again, I finished dressing before heading out of our room.

The common room was humming with activity. Men were up and about, the party seeming to be never ending. Though no one was drinking, and there were no women present other than Iris. When the younger woman spotted me, she smiled warmly, getting up and coming to me.

"I'm so glad to see you here, Winter. Do you want some breakfast? Blaze has it up and running. Should be out in ten minutes or so."

"I'd love some. May I take Serelda a plate as well?"

"Of course! You never have to ask for that, Winter." Iris looped her arms around one of mine and led me to a table where Sting lounged lazily. I knew better, though. He looked deceptively relaxed. He was very much aware of his surroundings, even if it was within his own clubhouse.

"Good to see you out and about, Winter. Is

Serelda well?" Sting stood and held a chair for me, then for Iris before sitting back down.

"She's good. Bit tired. She was still asleep when I left."

"I imagine so. You had a long day yesterday."

"Glad you came down for breakfast, Winter." Roman approached us with two plates while a prospect followed him with two more. The other man set his plates in front of Iris and Sting while Roman put one in front of me before taking a seat beside me with his own. "You and Serelda sleep well?"

"Yes. Thanks." I was so nervous there was no way I could eat. I pushed eggs, biscuits, and gravy around on my plate, nibbling at the bacon. I wanted to eat but was so nervous I couldn't.

Roman dug into his food, forking enormous amounts of carbs into his mouth over and over. He made it look so good I had to try a little. I was glad I did, because the stuff was delicious.

Talk continued around the table. Nothing heavy. Just discussions about the girls Sting and Iris had brought with them back from Black Reign. Girls who'd been in the group home where Iris and her sister had lived. Sting had plans for him and Iris to adopt the three other girls along with Jerrica. Which was where I knew Serelda and I could be of use.

I cleared my throat and wiped my mouth carefully. "Serelda and I could help you with them, Iris. That is, if you need help."

"Are you kidding?" Iris grinned broadly. "We can use all the help we can get! I've never been a parent. Not really, anyway. I've always tried my best to care for Jerrica, but two teenagers and a traumatized six-year-old are way beyond my ability to handle on my own."

"Not sure I can do much with Clover other than be there to hold her when she needs it, but I'm willing to do whatever I can. I'm sure the others are bad off in some ways, too. Knowing Serelda and I went through something similar might give them something they need to stay strong." I said the last softly, not really wanting to voice it but knowing it was the truth.

"I think you're very kind to offer so much of yourself, Winter." Iris reached over and squeezed my hand. She looked like she was near tears but didn't look at me with pity. It was more gratitude than anything else. Maybe this is what Serelda and I were meant to do. Maybe we could help these girls heal and, as a result, help ourselves. "Thank you so much. I'll be grateful for the help and the insight."

"How's Jerrica doing?"

Iris squeezed my hand once more before letting go. "Surprisingly well. She has nightmares sometimes, and it's hard for her to be away from me at night, but she wasn't hurt physically. Just traumatized mentally."

"I'm glad it wasn't worse for her. No child should have to go through anything like that. Are the others doing OK, too?"

"So far. They have nightmares too, but the one I'm worried most about is Clover. I have no idea what kind of past she has, but she doesn't speak and rarely interacts with anyone. Only her stuffed bunny. I think that's her imaginary friend, but she still doesn't talk. At least, I've never heard her."

"This is going to take more than love to fix." Brick pushed his empty plate back and crossed his hands over his belly. "We need to think about finding a good shrink for kids. You know. After the legal shit's done. Don't want there to be a chance of someone decidin' they need to be somewhere other than an MC compound."

"A solid plan." Sting brought Iris's hand to his lips and kissed her palm. "We'll do whatever we need to, so those girls get the right help. Can Stitches take care of that?"

"I'll talk to him about it." Brick scratched his chin under his beard. "I'm sure he's got connections."

"Good. Keep me posted." He and Iris stood, Sting taking her hand and leading her from the common room.

"You want to take Serelda some breakfast?" Roman rested his hand on my back, rubbing up and down in a soothing gesture. To my surprise, I soaked up the touch. Was I starving for affectionate human interaction? I'd never wanted anyone to touch me at Black Reign, though there were several men there I adored. They were more like older brothers or best friends than anything else. With Roman, I actually leaned into his touch. It surprised me how much I liked it. And those kisses we'd shared...

I nodded, not sure I could speak. I stood and reached for our plates, but Roman stopped me. "The prospects will take care of that. Come on. We'll take Serelda something, then take advantage of the warm weather and go on a ride. How does that sound?"

"I -- I'm not sure I should leave Serelda..."

"Go with the man." Brick stood and gathered all the plates, shoving them at a passing prospect. "He's just gonna keep at it till you give in. I'll keep an eye on your sister." He winked at me before leaving.

"Why is he so interested in Serelda?" While I didn't disapprove, I was worried he'd scare my sister. She'd seemed to be fine around him, but that could change if something he did gave her a flashback. It had been a while since she'd had one, but they still happened occasionally.

"Not sure. He's protective of her, and she couldn't do better than Brick for protection." Roman took my hand. "Come on. You ever ridden a bike before?"

"I rode with Rycks a few times. Before Lyric came back into his life. After that, sometimes Iron and Tank would take me and Serelda out. Not often."

"You enjoy it?"

"I love it. Sometimes, it feels like I'm flying."

"Good. Can't have my woman not likin' to ride behind me."

That brought me up short. "Your… woman?"

He grinned at me, and my knees nearly buckled. That smile was devastating. And was I really considering this? Why did it send a thrill through me when he called me his woman?

"Yeah, baby. I've already put the word out you're off-limits to anyone but me. Ain't no rush, though. We'll do this at whatever pace you're comfortable with."

I frowned when I really wanted to throw myself into his arms. "You're making this sound like it's only your decision. Like I don't have a choice."

"Not at all. It's *all* your decision. I've already made mine. Just waitin' on you. As I see it, my job is to convince you to do what I want. Then we're both happy."

The laughter inside me broke free. It wasn't loud or boisterous, but it was the first time in a very long time I'd felt the need to laugh. It felt better than I remembered. I shook my head. "You're crazy."

"I sure am, honey. But I promise you, you'll love my brand of crazy."

* * *

Roman

The next week had mild weather. Great for riding, if a little chilly. I bundled Winter up in a heavy jacket with my colors on the back, and we rode every day. Normally I'd never put my jacket on anyone else, but I didn't have a property patch for her yet. It was in the works, though. This was one thing I wanted no one to mistake. Winter was my woman. Mine.

We always rode through town at a lazy crawl, just enjoying the scenery. Winter had her arms wrapped around my waist, her face against my back. Occasionally she'd giggle or sigh. When she sighed, she rubbed her face against me like a contented little kitten. I'd never been had my chest puff out more in my fucking life. This woman, who was obviously traumatized, didn't like strange men, yet I'd managed to coax a laugh and a cuddle from her.

Oorah!

I was so fucking gone it wasn't funny. Yeah. I was good with it.

This was our thing while the weather held. It was late winter, so it didn't last long. I knew tomorrow the temps would plunge, so I wanted to make this ride last as long as I could. I didn't want to take her into the city, so I kept to the outskirts, just riding on the open road.

After a couple of hours, she tapped my shoulder and pointed to a fast-food restaurant. It was the first time since we'd been together she'd asked for something. I didn't care if she wanted food or just the bathroom. It was *something*.

I stopped in front of the restaurant, turning off the bike. She braced her hand on my shoulder as she climbed off.

"Careful of the pipes, darlin'."

She smiled. "You always say that."

"Don't want you burnin' yourself."

"You've taken me out enough times this week I know to be careful." She smiled at me. I got off the bike and took her face in my hands, kissing her lips lightly.

"Can't be too careful with you, Winter. You're in my care now. I'm takin' care of you the best I know how." She looked up at me with large, wide eyes. Moisture gathered in them before one tear spilled over and down her cheek. I smiled down at her, then pulled her close for a hug. "You matter to me. You matter a lot. I never want anything to happen to you, no matter how small." With one last squeeze, I took her hand and led her into the restaurant.

"I'll just be a minute," she said, pointing to the bathroom.

"Want me to order for you?"

She looked surprised, then bit her bottom lip, looking unsure of herself. "Are we eating?"

I shrugged. "Thought we might get something. They'll have a big supper at the clubhouse, but you've not eaten anything all day. We'll eat a quick bite here. Assuming, that is, you're not opposed to the food here?" I frowned. "We can go somewhere else."

"I'm not all that hungry, Roman. But thank you for thinking of me."

"Honey, we either eat here or somewhere else. Either way, you're eatin'."

Was it my imagination or was she smothering a grin? "Here's fine. Just get me a burger and fries. Something small. I don't need much."

I leaned in to kiss her cheek, and she allowed it, blushing as she looked around her. Was she embarrassed by the public display of affection? She hadn't seemed to mind earlier when I'd kissed her outside. Then she put her palm over the large scar over her cheek. She did a good job of covering most of the scarring on her face, but the one she put her hand over was long and raised. It must have been deep, and it was obvious she hadn't had medical attention for it.

"Tell me what's wrong." I tried to pull her closer, but she took a subtle step back. "Winter?"

"It's nothing." Her gaze darted around the restaurant. There were several people there, but no one seemed to be paying us any attention. She smiled, dropping her hand. "I'll just be a minute."

This didn't sit well with me. I hadn't addressed it with her, but it was obvious she was uncomfortable with her scars. It was still winter, no matter how mild the weather was, so she wore long sleeves. Her hair framed her face, covering as much as possible, and what was showing was layered in heavy makeup. It was a shame too, because Winter was the loveliest woman I'd ever seen. With or without her scars. I admired her strength and her determination to protect her sister. I never wanted her to hide from me.

When I ordered, the woman behind the counter looked me up and down like she wanted to eat me up. I ignored her, giving my order with disinterest. I could see trouble headed my way, and I absolutely would not fail this test. Winter would be devastated if I did, and I'd lose any chance I might have with her.

"You must be hungry," the woman said, twirling her hair as she gave me a megawatt smile. "Big strapping man like you. Bettin' you need lots of calories to fuel that big body." I didn't say anything, just stared at her. "You know, I get off in an hour." She continued to twirl her hair, oblivious to the fact I wasn't interested. "We could meet up."

"Just get my fuckin' food." I slapped two bills on the counter a little harder than necessary. More than enough to pay for what I'd ordered. I turned to the soda area to fill our cups. Winter rarely drank anything other than water or the occasional beer, so I got her ice water and myself a Coke. Then I stood away from the counter to wait on the food and Winter.

Winter came out before our order was up, and I welcomed her into my arms, kissing the top of her head. "You good, baby?"

She looked up into my eyes and smiled. "Yes. I'm sorry. Just a little self-conscious. You know. My scars." She looked down, but I caught her chin with the crook of my finger.

"No reason for that. You're beautiful, Winter. Inside and out." Again, I leaned in and kissed her softly. When I pulled back, her eyes were closed, and she had a little, bemused smile on her face.

She opened her eyes, her lips still parted, and she brought her fingers to her mouth. Her hands trembled slightly. I smiled down at her as she whispered, "Wow."

I chuckled. "You're good for my fuckin' ego, baby. Come on. Let's eat."

The girl at the counter had our food on a tray, ready for pickup. I did, and she winked at me. "One hour," she whispered. "I'll meet you out back."

I heard Winter suck in a breath and could have happily shot the bitch behind the counter. I leaned in and bared my teeth at her. "That's one. You don't get a second. Why would I want to be with you when I have her?" I gestured to Winter. Then I looked the waitress up and down with as much disgust as I could. "I'm not interested."

Winter's head was down, her hair veiling her

expression. I walked her to a table in the corner of the room. I wanted as far away from the counter as possible. If I hadn't known Winter hadn't eaten all day, I'd have just trashed it all and taken her home. But she had to be hungry. This wasn't much, but it would hold her until we got back to the clubhouse.

"Fuckin' bitch," I couldn't help muttering under my breath. This wasn't the worst thing that could have happened, but it was bad enough. I reached for Winter's hand and held it when she tried to pull free. "Don't." I hadn't sat across from her. Instead, I'd put her next to the wall in a booth seat with me on the outside.

"Are you going to --"

"No, Winter. And I think you know I'm not. She's just a spoiled girl used to getting whatever she wants. She saw my beard and tats and assumed I'd behave a certain way. That's all it was."

"I get it if you want her, Roman. I do."

I met her gaze and held it for long moments, hoping she could see the truth in my eyes. "I don't." When she finally nodded her understanding, I put an arm around her. "I told you, Winter. You're my woman. You think I'd let just anyone wear my colors? You've been part of an MC for a lot of years. How many men've you seen put their jacket on a woman?"

"None," she whispered. "The officers don't have colors at Black Reign, but the other patched members do. No one wears a member's colors but the member."

"Same here at Iron Tzars, honey. The fact that I put my colors on you for any reason should tell you something." I needed her to understand I was serious but wasn't sure how to do it other than to give her time.

We ate in silence. Winter mostly picked at her

burger and nibbled on a couple of fries. She drank most of her water, thank God. I knew she needed it. I could see her glancing at the counter, looking at the woman who'd tried to encroach on her territory. There was longing and sadness reflected on Winter's face that broke my heart. So help me God, if it was the last thing I did, I'd make her believe she was beautiful. And that she was the only woman for me.

Once we were finished, I helped her back on the bike before climbing on myself. "I need your arms tight around me, Winter. I want to feel you pressed against me." She did as I asked. I knew she would. Probably would have even if I hadn't asked, but I wanted her to know I needed her as much as I was sure she needed me. And I didn't mean in just a physical sense. Yeah, I wanted her body, but more than anything, I wanted her heart. Winter was the kind of woman who wouldn't give part of herself -- physical or otherwise -- to anyone unless she was all in. To be all in, she had to trust that person. I wasn't there yet, but I wanted to be and was willing to do whatever I had to do for her to realize I'd protect and cherish her with everything I had inside me. As a former Marine and the enforcer of my club, I had a lot inside me. I'd give everything to her and never think twice about it.

I looked back over my shoulder. "When we get back to the compound, you and I need to have a talk. You feel up to it?"

"I need to check on my sister. What do you want to talk about?"

"Your past. My past. We need to get everything out in the open so we both know what we're dealing with."

"I'd have thought you already knew about my past." She sounded small and unsure of herself. Not something I ever wanted her to feel.

"I only know the basics. You're going to tell me all of it. When you do, I'm never going to tell another soul. It will be our secret. But you *are* going to tell me. I need to know."

"Why? I'll still be the same person I am now."

"You will, and you're a wonderful person, Winter. We're going to be together for a very long time, so I need to know it all, and I want you to give it to me."

"I don't know if I can."

"You can." I reached back to gently squeeze her thigh. "You're the bravest person I know. You'll do this because I asked you to. I promise you we'll both be stronger for it."

Chapter Five
Winter

For the first time since Roman had taken me for a ride on his bike, I wasn't relaxed. The ride back to the compound was nerve-racking. The very last thing I wanted to do was discuss my past with him, but I suppose he deserved to know. I wasn't sure I believed him about us being together, though I had no idea what his game was. I knew it hurt like hell when that woman had come on to Roman, but he'd shut it down. I'd seen his expression. I'd heard his words. And he was taking me back to the clubhouse with no plans on leaving me alone. He wanted a conversation I didn't really want to give him, but he was with *me*. Not her. That had to mean something.

Once we got to the clubhouse, Roman took me to my room. "Check on your sister. See if she needs anything. If she does, we'll get it for her, then go have our talk."

I shook my head. "I don't want to."

"I know, baby. But you're going to trust me. You're going to give me a chance to prove I won't let you down. I'll be there with you, and I won't leave you. Get me?"

"Not really." I grumbled, but there was a flush of hope I wasn't sure I welcomed. He could easily break my heart and never look back while I'd be devastated.

As I opened the door, I heard a woman weeping. It wasn't a hard, raging cry, nor did it sound like she was frightened. It was more like the aftermath of a fright. Or relief?

"Serelda!"

"Whoa, there, honey." Roman pulled me back gently, putting me behind him as he entered the room first. There was no danger in his club, but Roman wasn't the kind of man to let a woman under his protection enter a room without making sure it was secure first. I had no idea exactly what I meant to him, but I knew he considered me his to protect.

"What are you doing? I need to get to my sister." Was I fishing? Maybe. While the need to get to my sister was paramount, I couldn't help but want him to be thinking of me.

"She's fine." Brick was on the couch. Serelda in his lap. She clung to him, crying softly. He'd wrapped a blanket around her shoulders and was rubbing her back up and down slowly, trying to soothe her.

"Serelda, honey." I knelt on the floor, brushing the hair from my sister's face. "What happened?"

"B-bad d-dream."

"Oh, honey. I'm so sorry." I turned to look at Roman over my shoulder. "I need to stay with her, Roman. We'll have to talk another time."

"I'll stay with her if you two got shit to work out." Brick hadn't made a move to let her go or to get up off the couch. In fact, he looked like he'd settled in for the duration.

"No. She needs me." Tears were leaking from my eyes. It felt like a punch to the gut to see Serelda so distraught.

Serelda sniffed, wiping her eyes with her forearm before turning to me. "It's OK, Winter. I'll be fine." She laid her head on Brick's shoulder and curled up on his lap like she belonged there. It was all I could do not to warn the big guy not to hurt her.

"I got this," he said in a gruff tone.

"You sure, honey? I won't go if you want me here, Serelda."

"No. It's fine. We came here to make a fresh start,

Winter. You were right. We both need a life. Because what we've been living isn't a life at all. No matter what Rycks said."

"He meant well. They all did."

"They hurt you, little warrior?" Brick cupped Serelda's face and looked down at her, holding her gaze as he gently demanded his answer.

"Black Reign?" Serelda's eyes got big, and she shook her head vehemently. "No! They saved us! They wrapped us up in a solid wall of protection."

Brick held her gaze for long moments. Was he trying to read her? Judge whether or not she was telling the truth? Then he nodded. "All right. Fair enough."

Roman urged me to my feet, taking my hand. "Come on, baby. Let's go. We'll come back later, and all of us'll go to supper together."

Serelda looked at me and nodded. Only then did I let Roman take me from the room. His quarters were down the hall. He unlocked his door and ushered me inside and to the couch.

"Here. Have a seat. You want something to drink? I got bottled water. Beer. Soda if you want it. Milk?"

"Water's fine." I sat on the edge of the sofa, twisting my hands together in nervousness.

He brought a bottle of water and handed it to me. I fumbled with the lid but gulped down a quarter of the bottle before setting it on the coffee table. Not only did I suddenly realize how thirsty I was, but I wanted to use anything I could to delay this conversation.

"Better?" He sat next to me and took my hand gently.

"Yeah." I cleared her throat. "Do I have to do

this?"

"Why don't you want to tell me? Ain't askin' for a therapy session. This is part of you. I need to know this to be able to proceed with a relationship with you. The very last thing I want to do is frighten you or hurt you because I don't know what you went through."

I sighed. "Can I ask you a question first?"

"Anything, baby."

"Why me? You could have any woman you wanted. That woman at the restaurant was sure interested."

"Don't want no one else. As to why? It's hard to define. At first, I felt protective of you. I knew you'd been through something and had no idea what. But I saw how hard you were fighting to break free of... something. You fought for what you wanted. You fought to protect your sister even as you knew she was struggling with being here, away from everything familiar. You did it because you knew it was what she needed. Somewhere in there, I realized you were the perfect woman for me, because you'd protect your family no matter what. You'd see to their well-being, even if it meant pushing them outside their comfort zone." Roman's words were so emphatic and strong I knew he wasn't lying. Everything he said was truly how he felt. How he saw me.

My lips parted on a gasp and my eyes got wide. "You really see me like that?"

"Absolutely, Winter. I told you before. You're one of the bravest people I know. And considering I was a Marine, I don't say that lightly. Now. You told me that your father was the one who gave you to the men who scarred you. You also said you killed him yourself. What about the men who did this? Did Black Reign take care of them too?" Now, Roman looked more like a killer. I knew he was the enforcer for Iron Tzars, but I hadn't really seen it often. Now, the enforcer was front and center.

"No. Not that I know of. I don't even have a clue who they were, and the only person who knew is dead. It was thirteen years ago. I'm not sure I could even remember what they looked like." I turned away from him. "All I really remember is the pain." I shook my head slightly before adding softly, "And the blood."

"I take it they were sadists?"

I shrugged. "No clue. They just liked cutting us. I think they liked the blood for some reason." I couldn't help the shiver as I remembered the feel of the blood covering my body. Both mine and my sister's. "There were two of them, but only one of them actually had sex with us. The other just… I don't know." My ears roared, and the room spun. I thought I whimpered but wasn't sure.

His body sliding over mine. His arms wrapped around me as he moved against me…

"Fuck." Roman lifted me in his arms and hurried across the room. The next thing I knew, I was in front of the toilet. Roman held my hair back while I retched over and over again, what little I'd managed to eat coming up in a violent rush.

A cool cloth wiped over my forehead, and Roman spoke to me in soft, soothing words. "I've got you, baby. No one will ever hurt you again. I swear it. Take a breath for me."

I gasped for breath, closing my eyes and concentrating on the wet cloth brushing over the skin of my face and neck.

When I was sure the nausea had passed, I sat back, collapsing against Roman. He reached out and flushed the toilet and handed me a glass of water from where it sat on the vanity.

"There. It's over. You're OK. I've got you."

"I'm so sorry, Roman."

"Honey, there's nothin' for you to be sorry for." With infinite gentleness, Roman pulled me into his arms and held me. Much like Brick was doing with Serelda when we left them. "Maybe this was a bad idea. I need to know, but..."

"No. I get it now. If something triggers me like this did if we..." I shuddered again, shaking my head. "No. I have to get this out. I see that now."

So, sitting there in the bathroom with me sitting between Roman's legs as I clung to him, I took a deep breath and began.

"There was blood. So much blood." I swallowed back the nausea threatening to bubble up again. "They paid my dad extra to be able to cut us. One of them said he liked blood play. I don't think Dad expected everything they did to us, but there was nothing he could do except double the price afterward. Taking us for medical treatment would have raised questions, and we were underage."

Roman's arms tightened around me, but he said nothing. Just kissed the top of my head and continued to rub my arm and back in a slow, soothing gesture.

"At first, they tied us down, so I don't like being restrained. Or trapped, really." I snuggled closer to Roman before I caught myself. "Actually, this is the first time I've been held by someone other than Serelda. There were brief hugs occasionally at Black Reign, but always by the women. I don't like men touching me."

"But you're OK with me holding you?"

I looked up at him and nodded. "Yes. It's comforting. And I liked it before. You know. When you kissed me."

He smiled at me, leaning down to place a gentle kiss on my lips. The contact helped settle me. I had no idea why. Maybe this man I'd built up in my fantasies and dreams was now my anchor. Though I felt gross and out of sorts since the vomiting episode, I couldn't work up the self-preservation I needed to. The longer I was in his arms, the longer I wanted to be.

"I probably stink like vomit and sweat," I muttered. I hadn't meant for that to come out, but I'd definitely spoken my thoughts out loud.

"You don't. Besides, good clean sweat never hurt no one. As to the other, it happens. Been in an MC long enough to see and smell it several times. You'd barely eaten anything, and it didn't smell like beer."

For some reason that made me chuckle. "Well, at least there's that."

"You think we can move to the couch now?"

"Yeah. Probably be more comfortable than sitting on the floor."

Roman helped me to my feet, then stood himself. "Brush your teeth and wash off so you feel better. Do you want to take a shower?"

I shook my head. "No!" I cleared my throat. "I mean, I want to brush my teeth, and I'll just kind of wash with a washcloth. I hate showers or baths." He frowned at me, so I quickly explained. "I don't like the feel of water on my skin much. It's thinner than blood but…"

"I get it." He looked like he did, too.

"I also don't like washing. Touching my scars."

"Do they still hurt?" He wasn't judging, just curious. Roman was truly trying to learn what made me tick and what set me off and why.

"No. it's not that. It's the sensation. I don't like

the feel of them. Even when I use something between my hand and the scars, I imagine I can feel them. I don't like touching them."

He stared at me for long moments. I got the feeling he was having an internal struggle with himself. When he finally spoke, his question surprised me. "Would you be OK with me washing you? I'll only get the high spots. Just enough to wash the sweat off so you don't feel sticky. Arms. Legs. Face and neck. Pits. I only want you comfortable, Winter."

This didn't compute. "You want to wash me?"

"Look, I know what it sounds like. But I ain't tryin' to get you naked and feel you up." He snorted. "At least, not right now. You were self-conscious about the sweat and vomit. I just want to offer a solution to help you have what you want and not be uncomfortable."

Tears welled in my eyes. Serelda and I had similar issues with water and touching our scars. She dealt with that part better than me, while I dealt with the nightmares and internal scars better than she did. "Serelda often helps me in the shower. She knows I don't like to touch the scars, so she helps with the washcloth when I can't move past it. I hold her at night when she has nightmares."

"Then let me do this for you. However you want to do it."

I thought about it. "A shower would be nice. Is that too much?"

"Not at all, honey. I'm here to do anything you need. Including getting in the shower with you." He gave me a cocky grin. Coming from anyone else, I'd have thought he was being crude. Not Roman. He was trying to lighten the mood.

"Before we do this, you have to know I'm not

pretty to look at. What you see on my face is nothing compared to the rest of me."

"Baby, there's nothing you can show me that's gonna make me change my mind about keepin' you. You realize that. Right?"

I sighed. "I'm not going to be that woman you're proud to have on your arm at a party, Roman. I'm always going to look like what I am. A scarred, traumatized freak with too much makeup on. My first instinct is to hide, not fight back. I'm always going to have a target on my back with any women at those parties, and I doubt I'll be able to hold my own."

"Like you did with Jezlynn and her group your first night here?" He gave me a challenging look, daring me to downplay what I'd done.

"That was a one-off thing. I was stressed to the max and knew I had to prove myself. I wanted to not be sheltered by everyone around me, and she said the right combination of things to set me off. Then the other one attacked me, and all the self-defense classes Rycks forced us to take kicked in. And the sight of the blood nearly did me in. If that had continued, I'd have lost my mind."

"Tell me something." He leaned one hip against the vanity and crossed his arms over his chest. "What kind of woman do you imagine I want?"

"I don't know. Someone like the club girls here? Like the woman in the restaurant?" I gave a humorless laugh. "A woman whose face isn't half destroyed by scars?"

"OK, so first, if I wanted that woman at the restaurant, I'd have taken the invitation she offered. I didn't. Second, the whores here are free for all. At one time or other, I'm sure I've had every single one of them. Every brother here has. If I wanted to be with one long term, I'd have taken one years ago. I didn't. They're for fucking before a man takes an ol' lady. After that, he works out what he needs to with his woman." He moved then, framing my face with his hands and brushing the pads of his thumbs over my cheeks. "You said you had no idea if you could move further than the kisses we shared together. Are you willing to try to do more? Knowing that I'll stop the instant you say so, no matter how far we get into it?"

I nodded. "Yes, Roman. I want to. I want to do it all, if for no other reason than to feel normal again. But I can't imagine trying it with anyone but you."

"Good. Because I've already claimed you. Once your vest gets here with the property patch on the back, it will be official. So, I want you to listen to me. Really listen, Winter. I don't want to have to revisit this." When I nodded he continued, "I. Want. *You*. No one else, Winter. Not the club whores, not the woman in the restaurant. You. Why? Because you're strong. You fought to overcome your past. You fought for your sister. You're fighting now for what you want. What I want you to realize is that it makes you brave, fierce, determined. You'll love and protect your family with everything inside you. And you have quite a lot in your heart to fight with. Not just physically, either. You did all this because not only did you need it, but you knew Serelda needed it as much as you did. If it had all been for you, you'd have stayed at Black Reign and been comfortable because you knew Serelda didn't want to leave. You didn't leave for you. You did it for your sister. You told me yourself."

He kissed me again, this time with more passion. It didn't make me feel trapped or like he was trying to take something from me. I could feel his need to give me pleasure he had to know I'd denied myself for over a decade. When he pulled back, I knew he could see desire shining in my eyes. Because I wanted this man. Roman. The enforcer of Iron Tzars. The larger-than-life man. My protector in all things.

"Winter, all those things are the reason I want you. The reason no other woman will ever do for me. If we never actually get to the sex part, I want you to understand there will *never* be another woman I go to. Not for any reason. We'll work on this together."

"OK, Roman." I smiled. Because I actually did believe him. "I believe you. I trust you."

"Good. I'll start the water, and you undress. If you want to leave your underwear on, that's fine."

"No." I shook my head. "I think I want us both naked. No reason to hold back at this point."

He smiled at me like he was... like he was *proud* of me? Had anyone ever looked at me like that in my whole life? I'd seen pity. Understanding. Kindness. I'd also seen rage, disappointment, disgust. Never had I seen pride. "This is why I want you for my woman, Winter. You're the fuckin' bravest person I've ever met."

Roman had said that before. Now, I was beginning to believe him. Not so much about me being brave. But I believed he saw me that way.

I brushed my teeth and undressed. I was slightly ashamed about certain things. Though I tried to keep my body grooming done, I wasn't very vigilant about it. And I never touched my privates except to clean. I hadn't really thought of that until I'd undressed. "Nothing to do about it now," I muttered to myself.

"What was that?" Roman glanced over his shoulder as he removed his shirt. Just like that, I could give two shits about anything other than looking at the work of art that was his upper body.

There was a tattoo of a plain Templar cross that spread the length of his upper back and shoulders. Around it were the words, "Honor, Shame, Death, Sacrifice."

"I -- nothing. What's this?" I skimmed my fingers over the cross, then the words.

"It's my story. My past. You want to hear it?" He gave me a challenging look, daring me to hear what he had to say. "It will change your perception of me. Not for the better."

"If you're trying to tell me you're not a good man, Roman, there's nothing you can do to make me believe that."

He removed his jeans and boxer briefs and stepped into the shower. There were more tattoos inked into his skin, but I was too preoccupied with this secret he was tempting me with to truly appreciate the art. Both the tattoos and the muscles flexed and bulged as he moved.

I stepped into the shower, avoiding the spray. Thank goodness the shower was the frameless walk-in kind. There was plenty of room for both of us and two shower heads. One was turned off so I could stay out of the water if I wanted to. I sat on the bench along one end of the shower, drawing my knees up and wrapping my arms around them.

"I was in the Marines. I told you that, remember?"

"Yes."

"I quit after four years in service."

That surprised me. "That's an odd way to put it."

"I should have been dishonorably discharged, but the Marines didn't see it that way."

"OK, that really doesn't sound like you. You're not the type of person to do something to warrant that."

"It was twenty years ago, Winter. I was a different person then."

"What happened?"

Chapter Six
Roman

I knew Winter didn't want to tell me her story, and I couldn't blame her. I didn't want to tell mine either. But I was serious about making her my ol' lady. That meant she had to know everything about me same as I needed to know everything about her.

"I killed a kid." I could tell by the way she sucked in a sharp breath she hadn't been expecting that.

"There has to be more to it than that. No matter how different you were back then, I can't imagine you doing something like that for no good reason."

"You want more? You come to me. Don't want to tell this unless you're in my arms."

She nodded and came to me without hesitation. Either she really wanted this story badly or she was beginning to trust me. Maybe it was her subconscious. Just like she'd let me hold her and kiss her before, she knew I'd protect her.

When she was in my arms, her face resting against my chest, I guided us under the spray before reaching for a washcloth and shower gel. She raised her face to look up at me but didn't try to move from under the spray. The only time she flinched was when I started moving the cloth from her neck to her shoulders and back again. As I washed her, I talked.

"We were on patrol in Kabul, preparing to reopen the American Embassy. Most of the people welcomed us, but there were a few who'd banded together to lead a resistance. Mainly supporters of the 9/11 attacks. The previous weeks, we'd been in firefights and such as the invasion started. They'd told us not to think of those people like we'd think of people back home. They'd driven out the Soviets twelve years earlier. If we weren't vigilant, they'd drive us out too. Kids were often used to carry explosives or to get close to soldiers to kill them, and I'd seen the truth of that firsthand."

I continued to wash Winter. I found the motions oddly soothing as I told my story. She seemed focused entirely on my words. She wasn't cringing away from my touch or the water. In fact, her hands rested lightly on my chest. I rubbed her skin lightly, but mostly I just let the suds slide down her body. I didn't want her focusing too much on my movements. Not this first time. Once she realized she could do this, I'd repeat it. Was looking forward to it.

"The only problem we had was some of the kids trying to loot. Even that wasn't a huge problem. They were just curious, like kids will be." I sighed. This was harder than I thought it would be. She already knew the outcome. The details shouldn't be that difficult. "There was one group of kids. They were more aggressive than most. I'd chased them off twice that same day only to have them return. The last time, one of them set off some firecrackers. That got every last Marine in the compound to sit up and take notice. It took a second to realize it wasn't rifle fire. The sound is distinct, but some of us were still pretty wet behind the ears.

"I caught sight of the little punk and gave chase. Naturally he ran, me yelling after him not to run. I chased him into the city, one of my buddies not far behind me. When we reached a dead end, he stopped. I told him to keep his hands where I could see them, but I said it in English. That was one thing I never respected up to that point. Most of the people there didn't speak English. Those who did spoke it brokenly and understood it about as well.

"He turned around and put his hand inside his pocket. He started to pull it out, and all I saw was the flash of something shiny. I pulled the trigger on my rifle, and the kid jerked, then crumpled to the ground. The second he did, the object he had in his hand rolled from his palm to the sandy ground. It was a stapler he'd stolen from one of the boxes going into the offices. A fuckin' stapler!"

"Oh, my God!" Winter looked up at me with horror in her face. "I'm so sorry, Roman."

"Don't be sorry for me. I killed a teenager."

"Roman, the circumstances were awful. And you'd been taught not to think of them as kids. Right?" She closed her eyes, rubbing her cheek against my chest. "I get it. I get why you shot. If that person had pulled out a gun --"

"But he didn't, Winter. He was just a kid. I realize sometimes sixteen isn't a kid anymore, but it doesn't take away the fact that I pulled the trigger. My buddy tried to get me to tell our superiors he had a gun, but I wasn't about to do that. I'd done it. I'd killed an unarmed civilian."

I stopped washing her, tossing the washcloth to the bench along the back wall of the shower and just pulled her into my arms before I realized what I was doing. Surprisingly, she didn't flinch. She even slipped her arms around my neck and held me too.

"My old man was a bastard. He fucked up all the damned time. Lost his job, the boss didn't like him. Overdrew the checking account, the bank made an error and fucked him out of the overdraft fee. Didn't pay the house payment, Mom bought too much needless shit. Nothing was ever his fault. He never took responsibility for anything in his life. I swore to myself I'd never be like that. So when I made my report, I told it exactly like it happened.

"My CO tried to take my words out of context, to get me to word it like the kid had been brandishing a weapon earlier that day or that I'd seen him with a weapon as he ran and he must've ditched it while I chased him. I clarified everything. I just… shot. I saw the glint of metal when he'd pulled that damned stapler from his pocket, and I reacted.

"In the end, I got reassigned back to Quantico -- mostly because I wouldn't let it drop. My CO told me I was being ridiculous, but also that he respected me for taking responsibility for my actions."

"What makes you think this will make me see you differently? I can't judge you for something that happened during war when I've never been there. Besides, it sounds like you had every reason to suspect that person had a gun. I think you're lying to yourself because you are actually a person with a strong sense of morals. But you can't beat yourself up over something like that."

If I hadn't loved the woman before, I knew I loved her now. She was right. My CO was right. It was just hard to forgive myself.

"You're a remarkable person, Winter. I'm lucky to have you with me."

She jerked back then, not out of my arms but to look up at me. "You? Roman, there is no man alive who would say that about me. If you look up high maintenance in the dictionary, my picture will be there! I don't know of anyone else who would put up with this. I mean, you've been with me a few weeks and we've only just now started moving in a sexual direction. And I have all these scars --"

I silenced her with a kiss. I did my best to keep it

light while still letting her know she needed to shut up with that shit. When I pulled back, I framed her face with my hands, forcing her to keep her gaze on me. "You are not your scars, Winter. And those scars brought you to me. If I ever find a way to figure out who hurt you and your sister, I'll annihilate them. But there is no way I look at your scars and think they make you less. You are beautiful, Winter. Inside and out." I kissed her again. "Now. I've told you my big secret. Finish telling me yours."

She let out a breath and slid her arms around me again. "I can't believe the feeling of our bodies moving against each other like this isn't sending me running screaming from the room."

"You sure you're OK? We can move to the other room."

"Just a little while longer. It's been a long time since I've been able to stay in the shower with the water… It's nice."

"Whatever you want, baby. Can you go on?"

"There's not much more to tell. They cut us like you see on my body." She stepped back and turned around, letting me see her front and back. Indeed, there were straight-line scars all over her body. Knife slices. Some were faint marks while others were deeper, raised white clumps of tissue. "There was blood everywhere. They laughed and played with the blood on our bodies. Tied us down… The second they let us loose, we clung to each other. The blood was sticky yet still slippery. I have no idea why I equated the feeling with water. Probably because when our father took us home, the first thing we did was shower. We demanded it. It was the only time we ever stood up to our father. We were in such bad shape I think it shocked even him. Serelda's face was so mangled, it took a very long time for me to deal with her. It was more than a week after our father got us back before Black Reign found us. By then all we could do was use creams and keep the cuts as clean as we could."

"Fuck, baby." I wasn't at all sure I wanted to hear any more. Thankfully, that was the end of it.

"Anyway. Bones MC had my stepsister, Darcy. Black Reign brought my father to Bones for him and our stepmother to answer for what they'd done to Darcy. They included us in that interrogation, because El Diablo wanted it clear that if Bones didn't deal with both of them, he had more than enough reason to do it."

"Then you took matters into your own hands?"

"I did. Weirdly, no one cared. I think Cain raised an eyebrow, but he just shrugged it off. It was then I realized Serelda and I would be safe with any of those bunch. We elected to go with Rycks and El Segador because they'd been the ones to rescue us."

We stood silently, the water gently raining down on us. She looked at me with such trust, facing at least one of her fears in my arms.

"So, what now?" Her softly spoken question was full of vulnerability.

"I hope you don't still think I don't want you, Winter. I do. And not just sexually, though that's part of it."

"Are you sure, Roman? Because I'm not sure I could recover from rejection..." She stopped, seeming to think over her words. "I was going to say after you made love to me. But if I'm honest with you and myself, I'm already too far in to ever be able to let you go willingly." There were tears overflowing her eyes, mixing with the water droplets on her face.

"I'm yours, baby. Ain't goin' nowhere."

To my complete and utter surprise, she smiled brightly up at me. Almost in relief. If I lived to be a hundred, I was sure I'd never see a more glorious sight than her smile.

"Roman." She breathed my name like a prayer, pulling me down to kiss her.

I took the opportunity to give her more, to show her I was serious about my attraction to her. I was getting ready to turn off the water when she pushed away and turned, picking up a razor from the edge of the shower with the cap still on.

"Will you help me? Serelda was always the one to help, but I want it to be you." She didn't look away in embarrassment though her cheeks flushed with it. What she hadn't figured out yet, but what I'd do everything in my power to get her to believe, was that I'd do anything she wanted me to. If she wanted me to shave her legs or under her arms, or anywhere else, I'd do it.

"With pleasure."

She sat on the bench, putting one foot flat on the surface, her knee bent. I lathered her skin carefully and dragged the razor over it. I was careful of the numerous raised scars and managed to do it quickly and without cutting her delicate skin. Her other leg followed, then her underarms. There wasn't an area of her body free of scars. Then, with a breath that was obviously for courage, she scooted to the edge of the bench and spread her legs. I took the opportunity to move between her legs -- I was on my knees on the shower floor -- and wrapped my arms around her.

I dipped my head and captured one nipple between my lips and gently sucked before licking with the flat of my tongue.

Winter cried out, her fingers tunneling through

my hair and clutching me to her. "Oh, God!"

"Mmmm…" I growled against her skin, moving from one breast to the other. "So fuckin' sweet."

Every movement along her sensitive flesh sent shivers through her. I tried to pull back to gauge her reaction. I never wanted her scared or to equate what we were going to do with what had happened to her thirteen years ago. When I did, she whimpered and pulled me back.

"Don't stop. Please, Roman."

"You tell me if anything I do frightens you or triggers you. We need to get out of the shower."

"Aren't you going to… you know. Shave me?"

"We'll do that next time, baby. I want to clip it first, so I don't hurt you. Besides, it may help you from getting oversensitized. Especially this first time. That will help you keep more control."

"I never thought of that. I guess it will feel different."

"It will. And it will be something we'll explore together another time. Assuming you still want to." I stood, taking her with me and turning the water off.

I snagged a towel to tie around my waist before taking another one and drying her carefully. Once done, I lifted her onto the vanity and snagged a bottle of lotion.

"You don't have to do that," she protested weakly, but I paused anyway.

"The feel of it bother you? You don't like the texture?"

"I -- no. It's not that."

"Then what, baby?"

"It's not that I don't like it. I just hate putting it on myself because I have to touch the scars." She smiled at me. "I'm just being silly. You've already done so much I just don't want you to feel like you have to do such basic stuff for me."

"You don't like touching your scars. I just shaved your legs. You'll be uncomfortable if I don't lotion you up. Can you do it yourself?"

"It's not that I can't."

"You just don't like it."

Again, her face flushed. "Serelda usually does it for me."

"Then it's my job now."

She nodded, and I continued. I applied the lotion to every inch of her skin I could, trying to use my touch as another tool to seduce her, because I knew she'd been enjoying herself before. Sure enough, by the time I'd finished, her breath came in sharp pants, and she was trembling.

"You good, baby? Too much?"

"What? No! Not too much!" She reached for me, and I wrapped my arms around her as she shuddered against me. "Why does this feel so good?"

"Because you want me. And I want you." I made her meet my gaze. Her eyes were glazed and glassy, the pupils dilated with pleasure. "Even knowing that, I'm not going to push you, Winter. You're in control. This only goes as far as you want it. Understand me?"

She nodded. "I understand." Her voice was little more than a whisper.

"Good. Let's go to bed."

Chapter Seven
Winter

I thought I'd be embarrassed and scared knowing I was about to have sex, but I only felt excitement and anticipation. Maybe it was the length of time between what had happened in my past and now. I didn't know. I thought it might be the man. Roman was perfect for me. He was kind and gentle, but I'd seen a more intense and protective side. Maybe not in a violent sense, but he'd certainly put the woman at the restaurant in her place. Though it had embarrassed me deeply that she'd ignored I was even there, Roman had stood up for me. Telling her he wasn't interested because he had me. I chose to believe him. I chose Roman.

He pulled the towel from my body and urged me to my back on the bed. He maneuvered his big body between my legs and covered my lower body with his torso. Then he picked up where he left off in the shower, lavishing kisses and sucks and licks to my breasts until I was writhing beneath him.

When he moved farther down my body, kissing my stomach, his beard tickled my skin. He continued to venture farther south until I realized where he was headed.

"Roman?"

"Shh, baby. Just one taste. I won't ask for anything more, but I need this taste."

I held my breath, unsure if I really wanted this. What if I couldn't do it? What if he...

He dragged his tongue from my opening, through my folds, straight to my clit. I couldn't contain the yell that burst from me. My fists bunched in his hair, and I didn't know if I was trying to push him away or hold him to me.

"Sweet as fuckin' honey." That deep growl right on my flesh made me scream again. My thighs squeezed around his body, and I moved my pelvis up and down, dragging my sex over his lips. He seemed to love the fuck out of it, because he growled again, sounding as elated as I felt.

I looked down at his dark head, his silky locks crushed in my fists, his short beard rubbing against my thighs. When he looked up at me with those piercing dark eyes, I knew I would give him anything he wanted from me.

Arching my back, I screamed as the most glorious sensations filled my body from my pussy through my belly. I had no way of knowing if this was normal or not, but I wanted more and was willing to do whatever it took to get it.

"That's it, baby. Give me all of you. Do it again."

I shook my head slightly, panic filling me. I wanted to obey him but had no idea how. Turned out I didn't need to worry about anything. Roman did more of whatever he'd done with his lips and tongue, and my body fell into line. This orgasm was slower to build than the last one, but no less intense. When I screamed this time, I arched off the bed, my whole body seizing and pushing through the pleasure. The edges of my vision dimmed, and all I could focus on was Roman, looking up from me between my thighs.

"Fuck me, baby. So fuckin' beautiful!" His low growl vibrated through my clit, making me shiver. Sweat erupted over my skin as I floated back down. My body finally went limp beneath him, and there was no way to keep the silly grin off my face.

"Wow."

"I'll say. I've never seen anything so fuckin'

beautiful, Winter."

When I could finally focus, Roman was moving from between my legs to sit back on his heels on the bed. Instead of moving over me, though, he crawled up the bed to lie beside me on his back.

"Come here, baby." He reached for me and helped me straddle his hips. His cock pulsed beneath my pussy as I moved.

"I don't know what to do." Insecurities were strong, but I was so lust-stupid I couldn't think of anything other than following whatever instructions he gave me.

"You do what feels good. Move your hips so your pussy slides over my cock."

"That's it?"

"For now. We'll get to the good stuff later." He gave me a wicked smile that nearly had me coming again.

Rubbing his big palms up my thighs, he moved them until they settled on my hips. Then he guided me until I picked up the rhythm. I looked down and watched his cock where it lay on his belly, wet from my sex hugging it between my lips. My clit ached and throbbed as it rubbed over the length of him.

Once I became more confident in my movements, Roman put his hands behind his head and smirked up at me. "Damn, baby. What a fuckin' beautiful sight."

"You're the beautiful one." As I looked down at him, muscles moved across his abdomen and chest with his every breath, making the myriad tattoos dance. I wanted to touch him but wasn't sure how far I could take this. My inhibitions were low, but there was still that little bit of sanity that held me back. "I've never seen a man like you."

"You've been in a compound with dozens of men like me, Winter. You just didn't look closely enough."

"Not sure it matters much. I saw you, and there will never be another man to compare."

"I'm all yours, baby. Now what're you gonna do with me?" Before I could think too much about it, I leaned forward, putting my hands on his chest. "That's it. There's no out-of-bounds for you. Touch. Kiss. Lick. Whatever you want to do."

Again, his words sent shivers of desire through me. It was amazing, really. That I was here with the man of my dreams, and I hadn't once thought about if he saw my scars. The way he looked at me said he saw me. And loved everything he saw.

There was so much I wanted from Roman. I wanted him to take me. To make love to me. To fuck me. I wanted it all. Was I ready for everything I wanted? I wasn't sure. Maybe not for everything, but I could follow where Roman led me.

"I trust you," I whispered. "Help me figure out what to do."

Slowly, he moved his arms from behind his head and wrapped them around me. His hands grazed my back up and down, drifting occasionally to the globes of my ass and the sides of my breasts.

"You're in control. This stops if you say."

I shook my head. "I don't want to stop."

"I know you don't. But if you feel pain, or panic, or just uncomfortable about anything, you have the power to stop this. I won't be angry. I won't try to change your mind. We'll talk about what happened and figure out how to fix it. You understand?"

"Yes."

"Good. Now. Kiss me."

I did. Greedily. I might be on top, Roman might

tell me I was in control, but I had no doubt who was in charge. Roman was too much an Alpha to not lead. Especially during sex. Honestly? I loved it. I was inexperienced by choice and needed his guidance. The position he chose let me feel safe while he was still able to be in charge.

"Reach behind you and guide my cock into your pussy. Just the head."

I did as he said. His cock was hot and hard, stretching my opening deliciously. I wanted -- needed more. He tried to keep me still, but the second I began to sink down over his cock, I wasn't about to stop.

"Baby, stop!"

"No! I want it!"

"Winter!"

Roman gripped my hips, but I kept going. The pain was fleeting and more of a burning sensation as I forced him inside me. I hadn't had sex since Black Reign had rescued me. Thirteen years. I was in no way ready for him and should have let him prepare me first, but I had him where I wanted him to be with all my being.

Seconds later, I sat fully on his hips. I could feel the skin of his upper thighs against my cheeks and wanted to howl with delight.

"You're mine now." I had no idea where the words came from or why I spoke them out loud. But I meant it with every fiber of my being. "I'm not ever going to give you up, Roman. Not ever." I rose before sliding back onto his cock again. Then again. "The club whores can't have you. Neither can that hussy at the restaurant. Mine." For some silly reason, I bared my teeth at him.

"Fuck. Me." Roman's eyes widened, and he got a slightly maniacal look in them. "You got that right, baby. I'm all yours."

"And I'm yours, too."

"Damned straight. Just let another man try to take you from me. I'll murder the son of a bitch in cold blood to keep you, Winter."

For some reason, his crazy declaration made me insanely happy. I lay forward on top of him, finding his lips with mine. Roman rocked his body from side to side until he found the position he wanted, his arms tightly around me in a comforting hold. Then he moved, surging up inside me in a slow but steady rhythm.

"Oh…" I gasped, moving with him as best I could. "So good. Roman!"

"I got you, baby. Just let go. Let it go."

I did. This time, the pleasure crashed over me like a tidal wave. I couldn't even scream, it hit me so hard. All I could do was hold on for the ride. There was no pain. There was no shame. There was only me and Roman. Nothing mattered but giving this man whatever he asked of me, because he'd proven himself. He'd taken something I never thought I'd have and turned it into the most spectacular moment in my life.

Vaguely, I heard his hoarse shout over the roaring in my ears. I knew he'd come, probably inside me. The thought was oddly arousing. His seed marking me. Claiming me.

"Fuck," he gasped. "Fuck!"

I collapsed on top of him, unable to move. I felt boneless, like a kitten plastered against a warm body. We stayed like that, both of us catching our breath until Roman rolled us so that we lay on our sides, facing each other. My leg was still over one of his hips, his cock slipping from my pussy in a wet glide. I felt his seed trickle to my inner thigh.

"You good, baby?" He brushed damp hair off my face gently, urging me to look at him.

"Better than good." I smiled. "Roman, I…"

When I couldn't finish the sentence, he gave me a quizzical look. "What is it?" A little sob broke free before I could stop it. His eyes widened, and he stroked my cheek again. "Talk to me, Winter. You have to talk to me."

"I love you, Roman." I couldn't hold back the words any longer. Until moments before, I hadn't realized the emotion was there. "I've never loved anyone other than my sister. But I love you."

He took a breath, then let it out, a slow smile gracing his lips. "Yeah?" All I could do was nod. "Good. Because I love you, too. I think you had me first time I saw you at Black Reign. Didn't want to admit it, but I loved that you couldn't seem to take your eyes off me."

"Really? You sure it wasn't my sister you noticed?"

"Oh, no, baby. It was all you. She only watched me when you told her to. You planned on leavin' with me exactly three days after we got there."

"There's no way you could know that." I wanted to be outraged, but an overwhelming sense of relief drowned it out.

"Do so. We'd just come from a meeting with El Diablo and Shotgun. It was right after Shotgun and Esther had located the transfer of Iris's sister to that fuckin' warehouse. You snuck into the meeting right under everyone's nose. You crouched behind the couch where you had a good look at me and you just… watched. Knew then you were up to somethin'. Also knew it was gonna be me who helped you. When you didn't make a move, I assumed you'd changed your mind. Then you turned up in my ride." He chuckled. "And you think you're not brave. You saw what you wanted and took it. A poor man like me never had a fuckin' chance." He grinned at me, still stroking my cheek.

With a glad cry, I pulled him to me, rolling so he was on top. Then I kissed him, wrapping my legs around him, so he had to stay right where he was.

"You're the best thing that's ever happened to me, Roman. This is the first time I've ever felt desired. I could see it in your eyes. You really wanted me."

"Still do, baby." To emphasize the point, he slid back inside me, rocking his hips gently. He pushed himself off me, careful not to trap me. The wonderful man remembered. He remembered I didn't want to be pinned down, even when I'd been the one to put him in this position.

Tears slid from the corners of my eyes down my temples. "You're so wonderful, Roman. I'm so lucky to have found you."

"I'm the lucky one."

Roman made love to me in slow, tender movements. Eventually, I pulled him down to blanket my body and was surprised not to feel the panic I expected. Instead, wonderful pleasure enfolded me. Just like his arms. He took me over the edge three more times before once again emptying himself inside my body. Afterward, he cleaned me up, then pulled me against him and pulled the covers over us both. I lay with my head on his chest, clinging to him like he was my lifeline.

"Just relax, Winter. I ain't goin' nowhere."
"If I doze off, you'll be here when I wake up?"
"I swear it."

Those must have been the words I needed to

hear, because I took one last deep breath, then promptly passed out.

* * *

Roman

I never thought I could feel so complete as I did when I was with Winter. The next few weeks taught me how much I'd been missing in my life. It also taught me how much I now had to lose. The more I got to know Winter, the more in awe of her I became. Not only was she kind, gentle, and the most fantastic lover I'd ever had, but she was wicked smart. And had more than a bit of a mean streak to her. Especially when it came to her sister. If Brick decided to take on Serelda -- and it was looking more and more like he might -- God help the man. If he ever did anything to make Serelda cry or piss her off, he'd have more than one woman to deal with. Add to it the fact that Winter had already proven she would cut a bitch, and Brick was definitely going to have his hands full.

Like I didn't.

"Roman." I turned to see Winter hurrying in my direction. I'd left her napping after a particularly intense round of sex so I could make plans for dinner. She was fond of Blaze's grilled burgers. It was still a bit chilly outside, but I'd conned Blaze into grilling for us. He did something special with his burgers that had Winter making all kinds of sexy sounds as she ate. I got hard just thinking about it.

"Hi, baby." I reached for her as she approached, wrapping my arms around her and kissing her. When I pulled back, her eyes were glazed and her breathing had quickened, but there was a look on her face like I'd distracted her from something important. "What's wrong?"

"I can't find Serelda. Have you seen her?"

I frowned. "No. I take it she's not in her room or with the kids?" The girls Sting and Iris had brought back with them and Jerrica were adjusting well. Serelda spent a lot of time with them. It seemed to be helping all of them.

"No." She wrapped her arms around my neck and kissed me once more. Probably because she wanted me to know she loved my kisses. She did stuff like that. It was important to her for me to know she enjoyed our intimate encounters with each other. She'd told me that several times, saying she didn't ever want me to think she was uncomfortable with what we did. While I knew her past still haunted her -- and probably always would -- she was blossoming into a very different and more carefree woman. The transformation was nothing short of miraculous. "It's not like her to go somewhere without telling me. Even if it's just to a different part of the clubhouse."

"She's probably with Brick." I should probably shrug it off, but I couldn't shake the feeling something was wrong.

"He's good for her. You think he wants to be with her, or is he playing the protector?"

I shook my head. "Don't know. My gut tells me he's interested, but I've not talked to him about it, and he's not mentioned anything." I frowned. "Though, I did see him in the common room at a party a couple days ago. Doesn't go often, but he usually parties pretty hard when he's at one."

Winter frowned. "You mean drinks?"

"Honey…"

I saw the moment when it dawned on her what I meant. Her frown turned to confusion. Then to something akin to rage. "I'll fucking kill him." She said it in a near whisper. I was pretty sure she wasn't kidding.

"You realize he's three times your size and a highly trained Marine. Right?"

"He has to sleep sometime. If Serelda found out…"

"She want him?"

"I don't know. Even if she doesn't, though, it would hurt her. Brick is one of the very few people she trusts. I get it if he's not interested in her. I even realize that if he's taken up the role as protector for her it's not necessarily because there's a romantic attachment. What I'm not sure of is if Serelda can separate her emotions from it. She may not acknowledge it, he may not realize it, but in Serelda's mind, Brick is hers."

"I get it. One thing at a time. Let's find Brick. Maybe he knows where she is."

I took out my phone and shot off a text to the VP. No response. That wasn't like him. Maybe he was in a meeting with Sting.

"I'm going to check her room again," Winter said. "Maybe I just missed her in passing somehow."

"I'll meet you in a minute. Gonna check in with Sting. Haven't seen him in a couple of days. It's possible he knows where Brick is."

After kissing Winter once more, I made my way to Sting's office. The president was at his deck, his feet propped up. Brick was passed out on the couch. The place *reeked* of whisky.

"What's going on?"

Brick grumbled intelligibly while Sting just frowned at the big man.

"Someone went on a bender the last couple of days." Sting nodded toward Brick. "Something's got him in a real snit this time."

"Not sure I've ever seen him do this to himself. What the fuck?"

"He's been sleeping it off for about twelve hours now. When he wakes up, I'll get answers."

"I was looking for him to see if he'd seen Serelda, but I can see that's not gonna work."

"No." He raised an eyebrow. "There a problem with Serelda?"

"Yeah. Winter can't find her. Those two always communicate their whereabouts. Even if it's just across the fucking room." I exchanged a hard look with Sting. "Something's wrong."

"I get that." He sighed as he picked up the phone. "Stitches, get to my office with some of that banana shit for drunks. I need my VP sober." He slammed the phone down and grumbled something about skinning Brick alive when this was over.

"I'd like to see you try that. He only lets you beat up on him 'cause you're the president."

"No shit? Well, he'll take this too."

"Ain't a crime to get drunk, you know."

"Not if it was because something went down with him and his woman."

That got my attention. "So it's not just me." Sting gave me a look like I was an idiot. "I'm not stupid, brother. I figured it out all on my own."

"Yeah? Too bad that dumbass didn't." He gestured to Brick.

"You're sure one thing has to do with the other?"

"Don't believe in coincidences. Besides, even if it doesn't, he's taken her on as a protector. He wants to get all rip-roarin' drunk, he finds someone to babysit while he does."

I winced. "Not sure I'd add the babysitting part where Winter can hear."

That got a grin out of Sting. "Or my woman. Iris would bust my balls."

Stitches entered the room with an IV bag of bright yellow liquid. "It's called a banana bag, and it doesn't sober up drunks. It rehydrates them along with other shit you wouldn't understand, and I don't feel like explainin'." The doc knelt beside Brick and tied a tourniquet around his upper arm before swabbing it with an alcohol prep. "Brick!" He smacked the other man's face several times in an effort to wake him up. He wasn't gentle about it. "Wake the fuck up, man."

"Whassup? Wha'der'ya doin'?"

"Fixin' to stick a big-ass needle in your arm. You move or take a swing at me, I'll jab it in your chest. Decompress a fuckin' lung or some shit, then leave you to die a gruesome death."

I snorted and Sting had to cover his mouth to keep from smiling.

Brick frowned up at Stitches, then looked around. "Where'm I?"

"My fuckin' office. You got black-out drunk and puked all over the bar. Didn't want my VP to pass out and drown in his own vomit, so I brought you here to babysit."

Brick stuck his chin up. "I can get drunk on my own. Don't need no fuckin' baby -- OW! What the fuck, man?"

Stitches had stuck him in the bend of his elbow with an orange-bottomed IV needle. "Suck it up, buttercup. I ain't waitin' half a fuckin' hour for this shit to go in. I got shit to do."

"What's that got to do with the fact that fuckin' *hurt*?"

"Normally, I'd use an eighteen-gauge needle on a patient needin' fluids. Goes in fast but isn't so big if feels like you're gettin' stabbed. Since I had to leave two of the most talented blowjob experts I've ever had to come fix your sorry ass, you don't get the courtesy of savin' you a little pain. You get quick. So I used a fourteen. Two sizes bigger than I normally would."

Brick gave him a hard stare. "Got no idea what that fuckin' means."

Stitches finished taping down the IV site and hooked up the fluids, hanging them on the IV pole he'd brought with him. "I can always load him up with potassium, Sting. It'll hurt like a motherfucker goin' in, then give him horrific chest pain right before it stops his heart. Detectable in an autopsy, but then someone would have to find his sorry ass to do one."

"Not until after he helps us find Serelda." Sting crossed his hands behind his head and leaned back in his chair. Brick jerked like Sting had struck him before bounding to his feet. Stitches reached out and shoved him back down.

"What? Where'd she go?"

"Not sure she's gone. Just can't find her. When was the last time you seen her?"

Brick looked away. Guiltily? "Yesterday."

When he said nothing, Sting prompted. "And?"

Brick scrubbed a hand over his face. "*And...* she saw me at the party."

"That can't be all of it," I said. That feeling of dread got much stronger.

"I was with a couple of the club girls. Didn't start out that way, but it ended that way. Serelda saw and..." He sighed heavily. "I didn't think the girl was interested in me that way."

"How could you possibly *not* know?"

We all turned to see Winter standing in the open door. Stitches hadn't shut it after he came in. Winter looked ready to do murder.

"She never said anything!" Brick tried to defend himself, but I could see it was a half-hearted attempt at best. He knew he'd fucked up. "I thought she wanted me around for my size. So I could scare off anyone she felt threatened by." Brick's obvious panic was cutting through the last of the alcohol in his blood, adrenaline taking over.

Winter stepped forward and, before I knew what she intended to do, slapped Brick with all the strength in her slight body. "You fucking *bastard*!" Brick looked as stunned as I felt. We all knew Winter had it in her, but I never expected this. Should have. Even given the seriousness of the situation, her show of aggression made my cock stand up at attention.

"Sexy as fuck…"

She whipped her head around to me, bringing her fury with her. "You think this is a game? No one hurts my sister, Roman. No one!" She turned back to Brick. "You better pray we find Serelda quickly, or I will cut off your fuckin' balls! We'll see how well your whores like you then!"

"We'll find her, honey. I swear." Roman was the one who spoke, though Brick looked just as determined.

"Damned fuckin' straight we'll find her!" Then, to my complete and utter horror, Winter burst into tears. I wrapped my arms around her, hugging her tightly. She'd told me when I hugged her like that she felt safe. Secure. I knew she needed that kind of hug more than ever now.

"Wylde!" Sting called out. The tech guy's office was next to the president's. Sure enough, the other man appeared in the doorway.

"Prez?"

"Pull surveillance around the clubhouse and the grounds over the last twenty-four hours. Need you to find Serelda."

"She leave the compound?"

"Not sure. Possibly."

Wylde nodded. "Not a problem. She got her phone with her?"

I pulled back and looked down at Winter. "Has she answered any of your texts?"

"No. But I didn't find her phone anywhere."

"I'll start there," Wilde said with a nod. "When I programmed her phone to have everyone's numbers I also put a tracker in it. If she's got it on her, it'll lead me straight to her."

"You what?"

"Relax, honey." I kissed her lips once to take the sting out of the tracker thing. "We've all got one. It's a safety thing."

Wylde headed back to his office, and we all followed. Brick grumbled when he had to push the IV pole, but Stitches just smacked the back of his head and told him to stop being a fucking pussy.

Once behind his computer, Wylde's fingers flew over the keyboard and clicked the mouse over and over. "Yeah. She's got her phone with her. Using the maps app right now. Let me access her camera to make sure she didn't ditch it." A few seconds later, he gave a crisp, satisfied nod. "There's our girl." He turned the monitor around for us all to see. Serelda was looking at her phone, then up, then back down. Then she went out of frame. Looked like she had it in her hand as she walked.

"Where is she?"

"Bus station. Not sure where she's headed, but I'll know soon. My guess would be she's goin' back to

Lake Worth."

Brick stood and reached for the IV in his arm. "On my way."

"You ain't goin' nowhere until you're completely sober." Stitches shook his head. "And if you rip out the IV, I'll put one in two more sizes bigger."

"No, I want Brick to go after her." Sting waved his hand. "He dug his own hole with this one. Time he buried himself in it. Send Atlas with him, Roman. Then you go take the edge off your woman before she cuts one of us. Stitches don't need the work when he's already in a bad mood."

"I want to go after my sister." Winter stuck her chin up in a stubborn tilt.

"I know you do." Sting acknowledged her but wasn't harsh about it. "You can go to her when Brick gets her back."

"She probably doesn't want anything to do with him anymore," Winter grumbled, but I could see she wasn't going to fight this. Which meant she knew Brick was the man for her sister. If Brick could get Serelda to forgive him and let him back into her life, I knew my brother would make things right with her.

"Don't blame her, honey." I fixed my gaze on Brick. "Sting's right, though. Brick ran her off. He needs to be the one to bring her back."

"We all good?" Sting looked around the room. Everyone but Stitches gave grunts or nods. Stitches just scowled.

"He falls on his ass he's on his own. And he better not fuckin' drive or take his fuckin' weapon or I'll make good on my threat to kill him."

"Noted." Sting clapped Wylde on the shoulder. "Good work, brother. Brick? You better fuckin' bring her home. And she better be fuckin' ecstatic to be here when she gets back."

Tall order, but if anyone could pull it off, it was Brick. I knew he loved that girl even if he didn't realize it himself. It might have started out with his strong protective instincts, but his feelings had grown. Right now, he looked devastated.

"I'll bring her home to you, little sister." Brick looked squarely at Winter. "I swear it on my life."

Epilogue

Winter

"I want to go after my sister, Roman." I'd kept quiet until we got into our room, but I wasn't letting this go.

"I know you do, baby, but let Sting handle this."

"If she saw Brick with one of your club whores, she'll be devastated!"

"Look at me, baby. Look at me." When I did, he framed my face in his hands. "Did she ever say anything to make you think she wanted Brick for more than a friend or protector?"

I thought back. "No. But anyone could see it. *Brick* should have seen!"

"I know, honey. But he's a guy. Either he thought she was just infatuated with him, or he was too busy taking care of her to see she had deeper feelings. Brick can be a dumbass sometimes with emotions, but he's the best man I know. He's VP because Sting and Warlock both trust him with their lives and the lives of everyone in this club. He's a fierce protector of what he considers his. My guess is he thought Serelda wouldn't be interested in him that way because of everything the two of you went through. His mistake was underestimating your sister. He won't make the same mistake twice."

I sighed. I got it. We were hard to read. Given we'd cut ourselves off from any kind of sexual relationships for so long, it was no wonder Brick was confused. I wasn't sure he could mend their relationship, given Serelda had insecurities as deep as mine, but he needed to be given the chance. For both their sakes.

"I love you, Roman. If this doesn't work out

between Brick and Serelda, I'm going to need to take her away for a while. Probably back to Black Reign. I can't be separated from her."

"I understand. I'll be with you wherever you have to go. Just don't count Brick out yet. OK?"

"OK." I smiled up at him.

"Now. It could be a while before Brick coaxes her back. Keep your phone with you in case she calls or texts, but come to bed with me." He winked. "I'll help you pass the time."

"Oh, you will, will you?" I stepped into his arms, loving how he surrounded me. "How you planning on doing that?"

"I'll have to show you. And you've got too many clothes on." His wicked expression was all the encouragement I needed.

Once we were both naked, he spread me out on the bed and pushed my thighs apart and to my chest. "Need my daily treat."

His tongue snaked out and swiped from my pussy to my clit. I arched my back, moaning loudly as pleasure engulfed me. I must have believed Brick was what my sister needed. Otherwise, I could never be here like this. I'd be pacing the floor losing my mind. But the big man was so protective of her, I knew he'd do whatever she needed. I actually trusted someone other than myself to take care of Serelda outside of Black Reign.

Then Roman covered my pussy with his mouth and plunged his tongue deep inside me, and I let it all go. I'd never thought I'd ever find pleasure in a man's arms, let alone pleasure like Roman gave me. I finally understood what the big deal was. The rush was as addicting as the man himself. Roman. My very own biker.

"Oh, God! I love you so much, Roman!" I screamed as I came, needing to let him know how I felt. Needing him to know he was just as important to my life as Serelda was. He was my rock. My salvation. The man who would take care of me and defend me with his dying breath.

"Love you too, baby." He crawled up the bed to cover me with his delicious, big body. "You want to be on top?"

"No. I want you just like this." I brought him down for a kiss as he entered me in a slow, wet glide. I whimpered as he situated himself, giving me time to adjust.

Roman caught my hands in his, lacing our fingers together as he brought them over my head. I looked up into his eyes, waiting for panic to seize me. When it didn't, I smiled at him in wonder.

"Roman? Oh, wow!" I shivered and my clit throbbed.

"You good? Need me to let you go?"

"No! Don't you dare!"

He gave me a cocky grin. Then he moved inside me.

Though he held me down, his movements weren't aggressive, and all I could think about was the pleasure. The excitement. I never thought I'd be able to appreciate the appeal of a big man.

Roman was everything I never thought I'd ever want in a man. Big. Scary-looking. Rough. Gorgeous. Yet I'd never felt threatened by him. Even when he'd been so startled to find us in his truck where we'd hidden, he'd been gruff, but I hadn't been frightened of him.

Now? All I felt was the love he'd professed for me. I could feel his love every time he touched me. In every kiss.

"Feel good, baby?"

"You know it does. Can't you feel my pussy squeezing your cock?"

"Fuck!" His body slickened with sweat, and his dick swelled inside me. "Yeah, I can fuckin' feel it."

I leaned up and whispered in his ear. "It wants your cum."

Roman arched his back and roared to the ceiling. My words must have surprised him, because there was no warning. His hot seed bursting inside me triggered my own release, and I screamed as I clung to him, my body floating on a sea of sensation.

"Fuck me." Roman gasped as he collapsed on top of me. He kissed my neck and shoulder as I came down from the orgasmic high he'd caused in me.

"Already did that." I tried to laugh but could barely get words out.

"Yeah. You did." He rolled over so that I lay sprawled on top of him, then pulled the covers over us. "I'll clean us up in a minute. Right now, I just want to hold you for a while."

"Fine by me." I sighed. "Best. Distraction. *Ever.*"

Roman chuckled softly. "It was."

"I might need more distraction later."

"Just say the word. I gotcha."

"This is real. Right? You and me? I didn't just dream all this, did I?"

"Everything about this is real. Feels like a dream to me, too, but I've already pinched myself several times and I haven't woken up, so…"

"At least I'm not the only one." I sighed contentedly. "I want to stay with you forever."

"Just try to leave. I'll follow and bring you right back to my side."

"Same for you."

I must have dozed off for a bit, because the next thing I knew, Roman was cleaning between my legs and pulling me against him to lay my head on his chest. Could life get any better?

OK. Yes. It could.

But that would be up to Brick. If he managed to make Serelda happy, my life would be complete. I'd have to wait for that one. But weren't all good things worth waiting for? We'd see.

We'd see.

Brick (Iron Tzars MC 3)
A Bones MC Romance
Marteeka Karland

Serelda -- Watching my sister find the love of her life has been bittersweet. As much as I'm happy for her, I'm heartsick because I can't have the man I want. Brick is my rock. The wall between me and the rest of the world. He protects and comforts me. He's everything I need. But he does it out of pity, feeling sorry for the poor, broken woman who sought refuge in his club. I have to find a way to prove to him I'm worth his time, and that I can be the woman worthy of the VP of Iron Tzars.

Brick -- The lovely woman whose name means warrior bewitched me from the first day I saw her. Serelda is scared and vulnerable. The timid sister. I know there is a thread of steel inside her, though. I see flashes of it when I'm least expecting it. So when she runs, though I'm disappointed, I'm not surprised. What catches me off guard is the moment she tases me. I might be a sick individual, but her show of aggression turns me on more than I ever thought possible. Now, I just have to figure out how to claim her without terrifying her. And how to keep her from being taken back to the very man who tormented her more than a decade ago.

Chapter One
Serelda

I'd never been so scared in my life, and I had no one but myself to blame. Getting a train or bus ticket back to Florida had proved more difficult than I'd thought. Orlando was the closest I could get to Lake Worth or Palm Beach, but once I got there, I knew I could call Rycks or Darcy to come get me. My stepsister had gotten closer to me and Winter over the last few years, but I'd still only call her if I couldn't get hold of someone at Black Reign. I felt too awkward asking her for help.

My sister. Winter. I hadn't been away from her for more than a few hours, and I already missed her like I'd miss my right arm. I couldn't tell her I was leaving because she'd insist on coming with me, and she had a chance at a new life in Indiana with the Iron Tzars. Roman adored her. Anyone could see it. There was no way I was going to cost my sister a new life I knew she desperately needed.

I knew I needed it. I thought I might have found it, too. Should have known better. Why would a man like Brick want to be saddled with someone like me? I was broken. Inside and out. Didn't take a genius to figure it out, either. My scars were the first clue. My face was covered in them. I tried to cover them like my sister did, but it always looked worse. Since I rarely went outside the clubhouse grounds at Black Reign, I didn't worry about it. Now, though…

I cringed every time someone gave me a pitying look, so I kept my hoodie up and my face in as much shadow as I could. I also sat in the farthest corner of the bus and tried not to draw attention to myself as I let the miles roll by in silence.

"Where's your pimp, girl?" A man sat next to me, moving into my personal space and mashing me against the window of the bus. We hadn't made a stop yet, so this guy had boarded in the same place I had. He spoke quietly, but his voice was menacing. My instinct was to draw in on myself, to ignore him and hope he went away, but I knew that wasn't going to happen. I'd always relied on Winter to handle people, but I was on my own now. And this situation wasn't at all safe.

"I'm not a whore -- therefore I have no pimp." I tried to keep my voice low, even, and filled with as much disdain as possible.

"Don't fuck with me, bitch," he bit out, leaning in close, his fingers biting into my upper arm as he grabbed me. He didn't smell unpleasant... exactly. Rather, he smelled like he'd drowned himself in Axe body spray, which was its own problem, but at least he didn't smell like body odor or sweaty feet. "I saw your face. Only one man I know of uses that scarring pattern." He gripped my chin with his other hand and jerked my head toward him, looking intently at my scars like he was inspecting them for authenticity. "Yeah. Looks like he got interrupted. Didn't finish with you."

"I was in a car wreck." It was a line I'd used a few times. Seemed like it might be a good time to use it now.

"Bullshit." He moved his hand from my arm to trace a particularly prominent scar on my face. When I flinched back, he gripped my chin harder and held me still. He traced one long, raised mark over my cheek that ran the length of my face to my ear. "No. This mark and this one" -- he traced another mark, this one between my eyebrows --"are precise and distinct." I knew the two he touched well. They weren't as deep or scarred over as some of the others, but they were carved almost like a design. There were several others over my body. Several more on my face. All of them in-between and around the linear cuts made by the second man.

"Let go of me." My heart pounded. Visions of those days and nights of hell flashed behind my eyes, making me flinch. My breath came in short pants and sweat beaded on my skin. I was headed toward a full-blown panic attack at the worst possible time. I was in danger. Any fool could recognize that. Though the bus was mostly full, no one seemed to notice my distress. On the plus side, as long as I was on the bus, this man couldn't take me anywhere. Sure, he could kill me, but I'd rather die than repeat the events of thirteen years ago.

"Oh, I don't think so, little girl. You're marked by the Cannibal. He only marks those he intends to keep."

"Well, he didn't keep me. You can see that since I'm here and my scars are old."

"Just means you got away. You're his, little girl. Reckon there'll be a nice reward for whoever returns you."

The man narrowed his eyes, inspecting more of my face before shoving the sleeve of my shirt up my forearm. On the inside of my wrist was a Roman numeral two the man had carved into my skin. My sister had a matching Roman numeral one on the opposite wrist. I'd never understood why he'd done that. Until now.

"Yep." He traced the mark on my wrist before going back to my face. "You're one of the twins he was so infatuated with. He's been lookin' for the two of you for a long damned time. Said the devil himself was protecting you." He looked around warily. "Where's your sister? And who's this protector even *he* wouldn't cross?"

"If you don't know about the Devil, perhaps you should rethink what you're doing here. I never knew who my attacker was, and it's been more than a decade. If he wanted me, and he hasn't come for me himself in all that time, perhaps there was a reason."

For the first time since he'd sat down next to me, the guy looked unsure of himself. Then he shook his head. "You may be right. But the money he'll pay me will more than compensate for the danger."

"You sure about that? Because thirteen years is a long time. I doubt he even remembers me." I was leaving my sister out of this on purpose. I didn't want this guy fixating on her and bringing danger to her home. "He might even be dead, for all you know."

"Oh, no. The Cannibal is very much alive."

"How do you know him? He's one random guy in one random city. There's no way another random guy in another random city knows the man who attacked me."

"First off…" The guy sat back, putting his arm on the back of the seat behind me. Anyone looking at us would think we were together. "I know him because I'm one of many men he has working for him. And none of this is random. I've been keeping an eye on you for months. Yeah, he's gone through several watchers, but he's known where you were the whole time." He grinned at me. "He's a patient man. Willing to wait as long as it takes for what he wants."

"Why now after all this time?" I was getting desperate. I knew the bus would stop soon. It was probably why this guy had approached me now instead of at the beginning of the ride. The very last thing I needed to do was get off this bus. But how to stop it?

"Because this is the first time since the day Black Reign took you and your sister away from your father that you've been on your own."

My heart sank. He was right. I'd run away from heartache straight into the worst kind of trouble. Had El Diablo and Rycks known all along the man who'd disfigured me and Winter would be looking for us? It didn't make much sense. There was no way anyone at Black Reign would have let that kind of threat live. Especially when he was most likely continuing to prey on others.

"So? We're on a bus to Florida. And if you think I'm getting off with you at any stop, you're even dumber than you look."

Instantly, the guy's face hardened. I felt a sharp poke in my side and knew he had a knife on me. The sensation made me want to vomit. Visions of a man standing over me, using what I remembered thinking looked like a surgeon's scalpel, slicing intricate carvings into my belly, my breasts, my face, filled my mind. My breath started coming in short pants, and I grew lightheaded.

"You'll do what I say, or I'll stick you right here."

"I'd rather die than go back to that hell, so do your worst, you son of a bitch." I hissed the words at him even as I fumbled for the phone in my jacket pocket. I just had to hit the button on the side, and it would call 911. That might not help in the short term, but maybe someone would know where to look for me long term.

I meant it when I said I'd rather die. In a way, it would almost be a relief. Sure, I'd feel bad for my sister. It would break her heart, but she had Roman.

She'd survive. But I was damaged goods. I wasn't nearly as strong as Winter. I'd seen that over the years since. She was the one to try to protect me. She'd been the one to kill our father. She was the one to move us away from the protection of Black Reign to another MC. One as protective but who hadn't seen us at our worst. I knew I'd never be able to adjust. Especially after seeing Brick with those club girls. The sight had shattered something inside me I knew would never heal.

The bus screeched to a halt, throwing me against the seat in front of me. The knife the guy had been holding against my side pressed harder, the sharp blade penetrating my clothing and scratching my skin. I had no idea how deep, but it made my panic worse, and I cried out in both fear and pain.

"What the fuck?" The guy turned his attention away from me. We weren't at a rest stop or gas station. We were on the interstate. From the looks of things, we were still in the right lane of a three-lane road. Other passengers looked up from what they were doing, some of them raising their voices in surprise at the sudden stop.

The bus started moving again, but off to the shoulder of the road. I had no idea what was going on. Had we blown a tire? Was something wrong with the bus? Maybe I should try to get away here. Hide somewhere and call Winter.

No. I couldn't call her. I'd call Rycks. He'd know what to do and could get me out of here. But how did I get away from this guy?

The door to the bus opened. The lights were out, and it was dark outside. A man growled something, and the overhead lights came on. More than one person complained loudly. I strained to see who was giving the orders. Because that growl sounded wonderfully, terribly familiar.

Heavy footfalls climbed the steps to the doorway inside the bus. There, larger than life, menacing in the extreme, was Brick. And he looked seriously pissed.

His gaze roamed over every single person on that bus, taking it all in. I knew he was memorizing each face he encountered and would remember everything he saw. Brick was brilliant like that. People often overlooked him -- even his own club -- because he was quiet and unassuming. Until it was time for him not to be. The club respected his brawn and unwavering loyalty. I knew there was much more to him than muscle.

During the time when he and the rest of his club, the Iron Tzars, had been in in Florida, I'd watched Brick intently. The club had come to help stop a human trafficking ring using group homes of orphaned and abandoned or otherwise unwanted children as their supply. I'd paid attention when the men had gathered around a table, poring over maps of the city and making their plans. Brick had led the discussion skillfully, planting suggestions in subtle dialogue until someone other than him came to a certain conclusion or laid out a certain plan. I suspected Sting knew exactly what Brick was doing, but let it happen. I didn't know if it was because Brick didn't want to be the center of attention, or if Sting was using Brick for his own ends, but I didn't think Brick was the kind of man to let anyone use him unless he was willing to be used.

After a long minute or two, Brick's gaze landed on me. He also took in the guy sitting next to me with a stare that should have sent the guy screaming straight to hell. The guy pulled me closer to him, the knife digging into my side even more sharply. I would have cried out, but I couldn't seem to catch my breath. Besides, I absolutely would not give the bastard the satisfaction. He might have brought back memories I'd have nightmares about for months, but I'd been through hell before. This was nothing. Brick might not want me for a lover, but he would damn sure protect me.

"He hurt you?"

"Shut up, you bastard!" The guy dug the knife deeper into my side. I was so proud of myself for not flinching or whimpering like he obviously expected. I set my jaw and fixed my gaze on Brick.

"I'll deal with you in a bit." The expression on Brick's face promised death. If the guy had been smart, he'd have pretended he didn't know me. But no. He was either stupid enough not to realize Brick was out for blood, or he thought he had a shot at getting around Brick somehow. He might have a gun. It would make sense that he'd pull a knife on me instead of a gun on a crowded bus. A gunshot would be noticed. Not so much a knife wound if he could keep me quiet. I had no doubt the fucker was packing, though. Men like him always were. "Answer me, girl."

"He has a knife in my side." That got me poked even harder. I didn't think he'd hit anything internal, but he'd definitely made a deep wound. I didn't flinch. "Says he's taking me back to the man who cut me and Winter." My voice was quiet and calm, but firm. Brick would know how it terrified me to even think about those dark days in my life. He'd held me after several nightmares and flashbacks over the last few weeks since Winter had started her new life. The knife the man dug into my side cut into me even more. I could feel blood tracking down my side, soaking my clothes and probably the bus seat.

Brick turned his attention to the man next to me, his entire being focused on the enemy in front of him. Everyone on the bus was watching the scene play out. I had a bad feeling Brick could give two shits who was about to witness anything he was about to do. Brick might not want me in a romantic way, but he was still fiercely protective of me. Of any woman connected to Iron Tzars as long as they didn't betray the club.

"Since there are women and children on this bus, I'm giving you a chance to back away. One chance is all you get."

"Stupid motherfucker! I'll fuckin' kill you!" Just as I was afraid of, the guy pulled a gun with his other hand. I shoved him hard just as he fired the gun at Brick. He missed Brick, but hit the man in the seat next to where Brick stood, splattering blood and brains on the seat in front of him. Screams and shouts filled the bus as everyone ducked. Brick hadn't backed off one bit. Instead, he pulled out his own knife and flicked his wrist. There was a soft thud and a gurgling sound. When I looked at the man holding me at knifepoint, Brick's knife protruded from his throat. The only thing visible was the hilt.

Everyone on the bus in front of Brick hurried off. People around us in the back ducked under the seats or next to the wall as close as they could get. A couple jumped the seats and hurried off the bus as well. Brick ignored everyone, shifting his gaze back to me.

"You're bleeding." It wasn't a question. I looked down and quickly turned my head away again. I hated the sight of blood. Any blood.

"It's deep, but I don't think he got anything vital."

"Let me see."

"Don't you think we need to get off this bus before the police come? They'll arrest you for sure! No matter what."

"They won't touch me. There is a bus full of witnesses to this. Someone probably got a fuckin' video. He killed a man, and I killed him to protect everyone on this bus."

That deflated me more than a little. Logically, I knew he was right, and that I didn't need to read anything more into it, but I wanted him to have been defending me, Goddammit! Somehow, I managed to keep my expression neutral even as I clamped a hand to my side. Hopefully, if Brick saw more than I wanted him to see, he'd think any pain in my features was from my wound.

He moved forward to the guy he'd killed and yanked out his knife, cleaning it on the man's shirt before sheathing it. Then Brick searched him until he found a wallet and cell phone. He put both in my backpack before reaching for me. He pulled me to my feet by my upper arm, firmly but gently, then guided me from the bus.

"The police will be here soon. Just be honest with them if they ask you questions. The fewer lies we have to remember the better, and neither of us did anything wrong."

"True, but you know they'll take one look at you and assume the worst." Police didn't tend to automatically assume bikers were innocent of any wrongdoing. Especially when they'd just killed a man on a bus.

"You let me worry about that." He had his cell phone out, firing off a text. Likely to Sting or someone at Iron Tzars. When he looked up, there was still no sign of the police. With a curt nod, he took my hand

and led me to his bike, shoving a helmet on my head. "Get on. Wylde says there's no state or local police in our immediate area. We have about six minutes before they are, though." He helped me on the bike before mounting in front of me.

"If someone gets a picture of your license plate, they'll find us easily."

"Taken care of before I started this chase. And we'll be replacing the bike soon, anyway." He started the bike and took off down the interstate, taking the second exit and the less-traveled state road.

Once he was on the route he wanted, Brick pushed the bike faster than I was comfortable with, but I said nothing. We were just north of East Ridge, Tennessee. About four-and-a-half hours from the Iron Tzars clubhouse. And, yeah, I wasn't stupid enough to think Brick was taking me anywhere else.

Thirty minutes into our drive, he pulled off the main road onto a smaller back road. From there, he took us to a barn nestled next to a wooded area at the edge of a field. It was nearly dark now, the full moon a pale ball of light rising on the horizon. The night air had a chilly bite to it, and I wasn't sure if I could make it all the way back to Indiana without complaining. I was already pretty cold, my cheeks and nose numb with it.

To my surprise, when Brick swung open the barn door, there was an older model Ford F-150 inside. He got in the truck and drove it out of the barn. There was a closed trailer attached to it. Brick turned off the truck and went to the back, opening the door to the trailer.

"Get in the truck, Serelda. I'll load this thing and be right there."

I did as he asked without comment or protest. I wasn't going back to Iron Tzars, but now wasn't the time to argue with him. I was as non-confrontational as they came, so I knew how and when to pick my battles.

Instead of getting back in the truck and leaving, Brick came around to my side and opened the door. When I gave him a questioning look, he held up a first aid kit.

"Let me see."

"It's fine, Brick. I need some gauze to cover it up until I can clean it."

"Ain't askin', little warrior." It always surprised me when he called me that. My name roughly translated to "one who protects themselves in battle," but not many knew that. I mean, why would they? It was one more thing about Brick that endeared him to me. And threatened to break my heart.

With a little huff, I did as he asked, lifting my shirt. It was caked in my blood, so I turned my head away, not wanting him to read my expression too much. Though I could take pain and be stoic about it, I hated the sight of blood. Hopefully, he'd think it hurt. It did, but it was nothing I couldn't stand.

He used a bottle of water and some thick gauze to clean the blood so he could get a better look at it. Then he touched it, squeezing it together and pressing against the sides of it. Probably making sure there were no obvious foreign bodies or maybe to see how the blood flow was.

"Needs a couple of staples."

"Good thing we don't have any. I'll have someone look at it later."

"Who says I don't have staples?" He opened his first aid kit and pulled out two packages wrapped in sealed plastic. One was a blue drape. The other looked like a plastic gun. Fuck.

"You're not using that on me."

"I'm not lettin' you sit here and bleed all the way back to Indiana."

"Then don't. Drop me off at the nearest ER, and I'll have a doctor fix it. I'll make up some bullshit story that sounds halfway plausible, and they won't ask questions."

"Not lettin' you out of my sight, either, so let's get this over with." That didn't bode well.

Before I could protest or respond or anything, Brick pulled my shirt up over my head. I'm not sure why I didn't stop him. I guess I was too shocked to realize he was actually doing it. I was sitting in the truck in only my bra and jeans. I gasped and covered my breasts with an arm. The arm on the same side as the knife wound, moving it conveniently out of his way. Brick didn't seem to notice. His focus was on the injury. Could this be any more humiliating?

"I think two staples should do it." He looked up at me. "Ain't got nothin' to numb it with. It will hurt, but not so bad you can't take it. And it's only two sticks. I've taken as many as five staples without numbin' the skin."

"Just do it," I bit out. "It's cold, and I want a clean shirt."

With a nod, he went back to work. He'd already cleaned most of the blood away, but he went over it again, this time using some antiseptic along with the water. It stung but wasn't as bad as the injury itself had been. The staples, however, hurt like a motherfucker. I managed to stay still and only tighten my jaw to keep from crying out when I wanted to shove him away and tell him to go fuck himself with the fucking staple gun.

Thankfully, he was quick about it. Brick didn't take time to do more than make sure the staple was in the right place and ensure each staple did the job of closing the wound, so he only had to use the two he'd anticipated. Once done, he washed the skin around the wound, getting more blood cleaned off and putting a bulky dressing over the wound before pulling me out of the truck to stand between him and the door.

He pulled out a pair of yoga pants I had crammed in my bag before reaching for the waistband of my jeans.

"What the hell do you think you're doing?" I'd never spoken to Brick like that. Or anyone else, for that matter. I always left that up to Winter. But she wasn't here. Guilt stabbed through me much like that stupid knife had. My sister was probably worried sick about me. Judging from the texts blowing up my phone.

"Gettin' you in clean clothes. The blood will draw attention we don't need."

"Like the mess of scars all over my face won't?" I shoved at him, trying to get space between us. "Move out of my way. I can dress myself."

He grunted and turned to face away from me. Not completely. He could still keep an eye on me, but it gave me at least a modicum of privacy. I stepped out of my jeans, draping them over the door of the open truck, then stepped into my yoga pants. I'd never admit it to him, but I was glad he'd had me change. I dreaded putting on a T-shirt because mine were close-fitting, and I already knew it would aggravate the wound.

Brick turned to me before I'd gotten a T-shirt out of my backpack. "Wait here. I'll get you a loose shirt."

"I'll be fine."

"You're not wearing a shirt that would rub against the wound. Even with that thick dressing, it could get it to bleedin' again."

I gritted my teeth but said nothing. His tone was

gruff and no nonsense. Like he couldn't give a fuck. I could only imagine how put out with me he was. But really, I hadn't asked him to come all this way after me. I was glad he had, given the situation I'd found myself in, but that was a fluke. If there had been any indication I was being watched, there was no doubt the club would have been all over it. They might not have appreciated that me and Winter had brought a psycho right to their door, but the mere fact that Winter was ol' lady to the Iron Tzars enforcer meant they'd eliminate the threat.

Brick came back with a huge shirt. He slipped it over my head and helped me thread my arms through the armholes and into the truck. *The fucking shirt smelled like him*! Was he trying to kill me? It was bad enough I had to ride in the close confines of a truck with him, but surrounded by his scent? No. Not happening.

I dug into my backpack until I found a larger shirt of my own. It was still tighter than I'd like, but it was a better alternative than wearing one of Brick's.

"You take my shirt off and, once you've healed, I'll be spankin' your pretty little ass, girl."

Well… shit.

Chapter Two
Brick

I was so relieved I finally had Serelda back in my care I was weak in the knees. My heart seemed to stutter in my chest, and my breath came in quick pants. I felt like I'd run a marathon. I was also so angry with her I really would be spanking her ass.

As I stalked around the back of the truck, I used the time to try to get myself under control. When I'd realized Serelda was gone, I nearly lost my mind. She was so fragile I couldn't imagine her out in the world by herself. Then when I found her with another man next to her, I'd seen red. Thank God I'd used my head and assessed the situation before I acted, or I wouldn't have had any kind of defense against killing a man in front of everyone. At least now, there was a bus full of people who'd seen him shoot first. I should have waited, but my gut was screaming at me to get the fuck out. That feeling had stood me well over the years, and I'd learned in prison to never doubt it.

After several deep breaths and a few seconds studying my surroundings, listening to see if there was a vehicle following us, I opened the driver's door and climbed in. Clasping the steering wheel in a white-knuckled grip, I sat there, needing to get going, but also needing to set things straight with Serelda. Without looking at her, I asked the one question beating into my brain. "Why'd you run, Serelda?"

I heard her gasp, but she didn't speak. Her body shook in the seat next to me. I could feel the slight tremble of the truck even though she weighed next to nothing.

"Doesn't matter." Her voice was a mere thread of sound. "You found me. Kept me from running any farther."

"I did."

Again, we sat in silence. I needed to get started so we could get our asses back to Evansville. But I couldn't. Not yet.

"Were you headed back to Lake Worth? Black Reign?"

"It's the only place I feel safe." She sounded lost. Like her whole life was gone. Maybe it was. At least, I could see how she'd see it that way. Her sister had found a man who adored her. Another person she needed other than Serelda. While that wasn't the way things were, and I knew Serelda was happy for Winter, I could see how Serelda would be uncomfortable.

"You don't feel safe at Iron Tzars? With me?"

"If I say no, will you take me back to Black Reign?"

"No. You're coming back with me regardless. You belong there. With your sister."

"Winter doesn't need me anymore, and I need to go back to my life."

Finally, I turned to her. She stared straight ahead, light from the moon bathing her face in an eerie, silver light. "You know that's not true. Winter will always need you. She's worried sick about you."

"No. I'm going back to Black Reign. With or without your help."

I clenched my jaw in frustration. We'd see about that. I started the truck, shoved it in gear, then headed off the property a different way than I'd entered. This was one of many safe areas the club owned from Indiana to Florida and in the eastern part of Texas. Most were places where we could torture a man then dump the body where no one would find it.

The next two hours were spent in silence. Serelda

didn't talk or complain or even shift in her seat much. But she was used to disappearing in plain sight. I'd seen her do it more than once. She could be so quiet and so still people forgot she was there. God knew I had. At least, the one time it mattered. I'd fucked up, and Serelda had paid the price. To be fair, I never knew she saw me as more than a protector. Now I knew she never would. And it was all my fault.

"We need to stop for the night. I'll get us some supper, then dress your wound so you can shower." Serelda didn't acknowledge me. Just kept staring out her window into the night.

I pulled into a roadside motel with parking along the back. It was on the state road, not the interstate, so I thought there was a good chance I could hide the truck. I shot off a quick text to Wylde, who assured me he'd secured a room. He'd been the one to suggest this place because it was relatively new and had digital check-in. No one had to see us, and he'd put the room on a clean debit card. The hotel would get their money, but if anyone pulled the records, the bank account belonged to a ghost.

Once I parked, I grabbed my bag as well as Serelda's backpack. She was out of the truck by the time I got around to her side, but I snagged her hand. I told myself it was to prevent her from running off at the first opportunity. And it was, I suppose. But I didn't want her running because she was afraid of me. Or angry with me.

Our room was on the first floor. I'd parked the truck close by, but in the back of the lot because of the trailer. I had to let go of her hand to use my phone to unlock the door. When I released her, I half expected her to bolt, but she didn't. Instead, she stood meekly at my side. I stuffed my phone in my pants before taking her hand again. Dropping our things at my feet, I shut and locked the door, all while retaining my hold on Serelda's hand. I had no idea why I clung to her, only that her skin felt good against mine.

Fuck. I was so fucking fucked.

Serelda tried to pull her hand out of mine, but I gripped it harder, not looking at her as I looked around the room and tugged her into the bathroom to make sure the whole area was clear.

"You think someone's found us already?" Her voice was so soft I had to strain to hear her, but she rarely spoke loudly. She was the quiet one. The one always behind her sister.

"No. But it never hurts to be careful."

Once I finished -- and yeah, I took way more time than necessary to search the tiny room -- I finally let her twist her hand free. She scrubbed it down her pants as if she wanted to scrub herself free of me. That made me angry. Lord knew I had no reason to be mad at her, but it was a blatant rejection of me. And Serelda didn't have that luxury.

"What's that for?" I pointed to her hand. "Think I'm dirty?"

She gave me a fierce look before ducking her head and turning away. "Never know where that hand's been," she muttered.

Right. The last time Serelda had seen me I was gripping the ass of one of the club whores, who was giving me a lap dance. I hadn't fucked the bitch. I'd been so drunk I'm not sure I could have fucked her. It was the only reason I'd been in that position in the first Goddamned place. The damage had been done, though. I'd spotted Serelda the second she'd spotted me. Our gazes locked, and the hurt on her face had been like a kick to the balls. She'd left the room immediately. I'd tried to follow her but had ended up falling into the lap of one of my brothers. Literally. Someone had helped me to my room -- and by helped, I mean carried my drunk ass -- and I'd passed out for the rest of the night. It hadn't been long after that Winter had discovered her sister missing. I'm not sure I'd ever felt more like a failure than I had then. I'd known Serelda was fragile, but I'd felt more for her than the simple need to protect her, and I didn't think there was any way Serelda would be up for that.

"It ain't been nowhere," I growled at her. "Even if it was, I don't have to explain myself to you."

"You're right," she said, still not meeting my gaze but digging through her bag for clean clothes. "You don't. Just like I don't have to explain where I'm going or why."

"You do when I have to kill a man to get you out of the situation you're in."

"No one asked you to do that, Brick. In fact, I don't want or need your help any longer. I'll have Rycks send someone for me. Black Reign will compensate you for this room."

I narrowed my eyes at her. Serelda was the delicate one. I'd always treated her as such, but the terror I'd experienced knowing that fuckhead had a knife on her had my hackles rising. I'd killed the bastard too quickly and was spoiling for a fight to relieve some tension. The last thing she needed was for me to take out my anger on her when it wasn't her fault. Sure, she'd left, but I was angry at myself for caring she'd left. Sting was the only person I'd ever concerned myself with protecting. He was not only my president, but my best friend. The one man who'd stood by me since I'd gotten out of prison six years ago. Now, I'd gone and attached myself to this woman and had no idea how it had even happened.

"You seem pretty sure you can get another club to pay your tab. Is that what you do? Run from club to club looking for someone to take care of you?" The second I uttered the words, I knew I'd fucked up. Serelda's expression shut down. She turned her back to me. When she whipped back around, it was with a Taser in her hand. She pointed it at me and fired without a moment's hesitation.

The darts hit my chest with a little sting. Then my whole body seized, my muscles stiffening as the electric shock scrambled my nervous system. I tried to power through it, but there was no fighting the effects. Lord knew I'd gone through this more than once in prison. The best thing I could do was to let it have me. The more I fought, the more my body would hurt later.

Serelda yanked at the wires coming from her Taser, pulling the attached darts from my chest. As she passed, she kicked my stomach. Hard. Backpack slung over her shoulder, she stomped past my sorry hide and to the door.

"Serelda, stop!" My voice wasn't nearly strong enough to give that kind of command and expect her to obey me. And, of course, she didn't. Unlocking the door, she flung it open and hurried outside.

It took me several seconds to gather myself. My muscles ached like I'd been run over by a fucking truck. Finally, I managed to stumble to my feet and outside. I saw her form rounding the corner of the building and hurried off in that direction. Well, I moved as fast as I could. Which wasn't saying much. My legs still didn't want to work. Sheer force of will was all that kept me going.

I found her in the lobby, where she'd ducked behind a plant. She had her phone to her ear, and I heard her telling someone where she was and promising to keep her phone on so they could track her. When she saw me, she gave a little squeak and scrambled back farther. I reached out and snagged the phone, putting it to my ear.

"Who the fuck is this?" I was in no position to demand anything, but it went against my nature to do anything but demand in certain circumstances.

"Rycks. Who the fuck is this?"

"I've got everything under control," I bit out, not answering his question. "I'll take her back to Iron Tzars and everything will be fucking fine."

"Brick? What the fuck, man? You sound like you're ready to throttle someone. What happened?"

"None of your Goddamn business. I got this."

"I'm making it my business." The other man went from mildly irritated and slightly disbelieving to pissed the fuck off in two point three seconds. "Now tell me what the fuck happened."

"Your girl went and got herself in some trouble. I rescued her." That was all he was getting over a questionable connection. I didn't think they'd put me back in prison for killing a guy in self-defense, but I wasn't going to admit to anything on my own.

"So why do you sound so surly?"

"Rough fuckin' day. She's fine. I got this." I ended the call before he could continue. Then I snagged Serelda's hand again and marched her out the door. "You do that again, you're goin' over my knee. After that, I promise you won't ever do it again."

"Are you threatening me? Because I warn you, you may get the better of me now, but you have to sleep sometime."

I gave her an annoyed glance as we entered the room once more. I locked it and pulled the drapes.

"Why in the fuck I pegged you as the quiet one who needed handling with kid gloves is beyond me. You're a fuckin' hell cat."

She lifted her chin. When she did, she must have caught a glimpse of her reflection in the mirror, because she gave a little gasp. After several seconds, she ducked her head and turned away from me. I wanted to stay mad. Needed to keep her at arm's length. But that glimpse of the warrior she'd shown me now vanished right before my eyes, and Serelda was once again a broken, terrified woman. I needed to make it better. Strangely, I wanted to spar with that warrior she'd shown me. It let me know she was back with the living instead of trapped in her nightmare past.

Carefully, I stepped toward her, putting my hands on her shoulders. She flinched but allowed the contact. "I'm sorry, Serelda. It's been a long day, and I think I'm more worried about blowback from killin' that fucker than I wanted to admit."

"Not your fault." She dug back into her bag and pulled out some soft pants and a T-shirt along with underwear. "I'm going to freshen up." With that, Serelda shrugged my hands away and darted into the bathroom. Soon after, I heard the water in the shower running. I wanted to follow her. Make sure she was OK. But I didn't dare. Not only would she resent it, but I was terribly afraid I wouldn't be able to keep things non-personal if I did.

* * *

Serelda

Once I was safely behind a locked door and in the shower, I let go. I sobbed as quietly as I could, but the tears came and wouldn't let up. I stuffed the washcloth in my mouth to muffle my cries, because I knew if Brick heard me, he'd break the door down to get to me. At least, that's what he would have done before I ran. But he would have done it out of pity. Not because he saw me as a woman he wanted.

Goddammit! I was sick and fucking tired of being treated like I was broken, even if I was. I didn't want to be this way! I wanted to have what Winter had. A chance at a new life. Then I'd catch a look at myself in the mirror and remember there was no way anyone wanted a woman as scarred and damaged as me. I'd thought Brick was different. Even thought I was growing to love him. Other than Serelda, he'd been the only person to make me feel like I wasn't a burden. Even when he'd had to take time out of his day to calm my fears or sit quietly with me so I wasn't alone, I'd thought he'd wanted to be with me. I'd thought that maybe he enjoyed my company as much as I did his. When I was with him, I felt a peace and security I'd never had before. Not even with Black Reign. Then I'd seen him at the party with one of the women in the compound. I had no right to be jealous, but I was. And it had hurt like nothing else in my life. Not even what I'd gone through in my past had compared to seeing Brick with another woman.

It took a long time for me to get myself under control. I sat on the floor of the shower and let it all out, because I knew if I didn't, it would break free at a time when it would embarrass me. Like in front of Brick.

Thankfully, the storm passed before Brick decided I'd been in there long enough and started pounding on the door. I didn't get myself under control so much as I was finally... *empty*. The emotions I'd tried so hard to hold back had burst free. I didn't feel good, but I felt better about the situation. I knew I could hold myself together for a while longer. The knock at the door told me my reprieve was over.

"Serelda, honey. Open the door."

"I'm in the shower. I'll open the door when I'm decent."

"You've been in there an hour." He didn't sound angry. In fact, he could have been talking about the weather for all the emotion in his voice. That was Brick. He didn't have to show emotion. His size and the fierce scowl on his face most of the time made people do what he wanted.

"And I'll be in here another hour if I choose. Go away."

"I'm given' you five more minutes, then I'm comin' in after you."

He would, too. I wanted to punch something. "Why can't you be happy I'm in the stupid room? There's no window, so I can't escape. Let me have some peace and quiet for a while!"

"You've been alone with your peace and quiet for far too fuckin' long, Serelda. Get your pretty ass out here. It's time for bed. I've been chasin' you all fuckin' day, and I ain't goin' to sleep until you're out here with me."

"Stubborn-ass man," I grumbled. I knew he'd keep at it until that five minutes was up. Then he'd probably break the door down. Given I had no idea if anyone had followed us or not, I didn't want to draw attention to him by having the police called if someone thought there was a fight going on.

I turned off the water and snagged a towel. My skin was pruned from the hot water, but after my cry, I felt much better. I thought I could make it through this. Tomorrow, he'd take me back to the Tzars, and I'd call Rycks to come get me in Indiana. Brick might win this battle, but I would win the war.

After dressing, I grabbed a clean towel to wrap my hair in. I opened the door to find Brick standing on the other side. I looked up at him, and my heart stuttered. The man was insufferably gorgeous. At least, he was to me.

His hair was shaved on the sides, but long on top, making for a shaggy mess I longed to run my fingers through. His beard was white at the chin and temples, with more white sprinkled liberally through the rest of the dark mass. He was tall -- well over six feet -- with wide, thick shoulders and a muscled chest, all of which strained the T-shirt he wore. Brawny forearms were covered with tattoos, most of which looked like prison tattoos. I seemed to vaguely remember someone saying he'd done some time, but I hadn't wanted to pry.

"Feel better?" His voice was rumbly and deep. It always soothed me when I woke up from a nightmare. Now, it made a fresh wave of tears try to overtake me. I fought them back by sheer force of will, because I absolutely would not let this man see me cry. Not over him.

"Yes." I pushed past him and went to my bag, retrieving my hairbrush. More than once, Brick had brushed the tangles from my hair. Usually after I'd had to take a shower to wash off the sweat after a nightmare or a panic attack. Why had the man taken such good care of me when he wasn't interested in me? I mean, I got why he didn't want me sexually. What man would want to look at all these stupid scars on a regular basis? But why had he acted like he cared so much?

"Here." He reached out and plucked the brush from my hand. "Sit on the bed. I'll brush your hair for you."

"I can do it myself." I tried to take back the brush, but he raised an eyebrow and held it out of reach.

"I know you can, but you're going to let me. Now. On the bed, please."

I huffed and plopped down on the bed in a disgruntled heap, arms crossed over my breasts. I heard Brick sigh behind me. He moved so that he sat leaning against the headboard with me between his legs. We'd sat like this often while he did this exact same thing. Then he moved the brush to the top of my head and stroked downward in careful, gentle slides.

Moisture sprang to my eyes. This was the one gesture Brick made that even Winter had never done for me. As tears slid down my face in silent tracks, I remembered the first night we'd done this. I'd had a breakdown after a flashback, and Brick comforted me exactly like this. Since that night, this was a ritual he'd insisted on.

Without so much as snagging a single hair enough to cause pain, he would detangle my hair and brush the long, thick mass until it was dry. It sometimes took as much as an hour. Sometimes we talked. Sometimes we sat in silence. Always it soothed me when nothing else could. But only with Brick.

That was the problem. Brick was mine in every way but the one that mattered. I wasn't sure if I'd ever be ready for that, or if he was even willing to wait, if he'd wanted me at all. Hell, the man saw me as nothing more than a woman to be coddled but pitied. No man would want a woman like that for his own. Especially not a man as strong as Brick. He'd need a woman equal in strength at his side. One who could help him in his club. Not break down in tears after a stupid nightmare. So the reality was, I was his, but he wasn't mine. It felt like I had a hopeless crush on Brick. One he had no way of returning, because I could never be what he needed.

Little by little, the tension faded from my body. My mind focused on nothing but the next brush stroke. Lethargy wrapped around me like a warm, fuzzy blanket, and I was nearly asleep where I sat. It was like I was in a trance. Waiting for the next stroke of the brush.

I must have dozed off because the next thing I knew, Brick was moving me so that I lay with my back to his chest. He reached over and switched off the light before settling on his side, my head pillowed on one arm while he wrapped the other one around me. He shifted once to pull me more solidly against him, then was still. The warmth and security were an extra layer of comfort, and there was no way I could fight against sleep. With a sigh, I closed my eyes and let it take me.

Chapter Three
Serelda

I woke up needing the bathroom. It didn't seem like I'd moved a muscle. Brick's big, solid body was still snug behind me, and his brawny arm wrapped around me. The only difference was, the arm my head was pillowed on was also wrapped around me. I'm not sure I'd ever felt so safe and warm as I did in that moment.

Despite needing to get up, I found myself drifting, allowing myself to imagine this same setting but with a different scenario. What if Brick claimed me as his? What if he wanted me the way I wanted him? He could be wrapped around me like this after a night of lovemaking. Or because he genuinely wanted to be with me instead of trying to keep me from running off or to calm my fears.

There was nothing more I wanted to do than stay right where I was. And I tried! But my bladder was having none of it, and I had to get up to take care of business.

Brick grunted, his arms tightening slightly before letting me go. "Where're you goin'?" God, his voice was sexy roughened from sleep! Made me wonder if he'd sound like that if he bellowed to the rafters as he came... *deep inside me...*

"Bathroom." My voice was husky, and I suspected it wasn't only because I'd been asleep. I was more turned-on than I had ever been in my life. Even before my father had sold me and Winter to sadistic bastards to use as they pleased. Before I hadn't been old enough to know what sex really was. After, I hadn't wanted to be touched by a man ever again. Now? I still didn't want to be touched. Except by Brick.

I wanted him to touch me more than I wanted to take my next breath.

He growled once, then kissed the delicate skin behind my ear. "You come right back. Ain't time to get up."

Instead of answering, I scrambled out of bed and hurried to the bathroom. The urge to retreat again like I had before was strong, but I knew Brick wouldn't allow it. Sure enough, ten minutes later, there was a knock at the door.

"You ain't stayin' in there the rest of the night, little warrior." He knocked again for emphasis. "Come on."

I opened the door, suddenly shy about seeing him. I'd acknowledged to myself I wanted Brick, but I wasn't sure I was ready to face the reality that he'd never see me that way. I ducked my head, but Brick caught my chin and gently forced my head up so he could look down into my eyes. There was only a nightlight where the light switch was. The curtains in the room were pulled, and I'd turned the light in the bathroom off before I'd opened the door. I had no idea what he thought he could see, but I was grateful for the lack of lighting.

"We need to get a few things straight, little warrior."

"Why do you keep calling me that?"

"Because it's what you are. And no. It's not because of your name. I know what your name means, but that's not why you're a warrior."

"I'm not a warrior, and I know you know it."

"Oh?" He tilted his head as he continued to look down into my face. I wished I could see his expression. The reddish-orange glow of the safety light on the light switch wasn't enough to get a good read on him. "Why would you say that?"

I snorted, turning my head to free myself from his fingers. He refused to let me go and stepped closer into my personal space in a slow, deliberate step. If it had been anyone other than Brick moving in on me like he was, in a dominant position holding my head still, I'd have backed up and tried to get away. With Brick, I not only held my ground, but stepped forward, closing the scant inches separating us. His arm slid around me to palm my back with his big hand. It nearly covered the entire surface. Instead of panicking, I inhaled deeply of his scent. It was comforting. Just like it had been when I'd lain in his arms on the bed.

"You've been fighting an internal war half your life. You didn't give up. You fought for your sister. And yourself. I know if it hadn't been Winter wanting to leave the safety of Black Reign, you'd never have done it on your own. You did it because Winter needed it."

"She only did it because she thought it was what was best for me. She'd have stayed if not for me."

"Honey, she left for you. You left for her. You both fought for each other and pushed through your fears to help your family. In my book, that makes you the fiercest warriors of all."

I couldn't help the little sob that escaped me. Did he really see me like that? "I'm not brave, Brick. I hid myself away after Black Reign found Winter and me, and I've been licking my wounds ever since."

"So? Everyone needs time to recover."

"Even you? And if you tell me yes, then I'll call you a Goddamn liar. You aren't the type of man to hide from anything."

Brick let go of my face to wrap his other arm around me in a tight hug. God, I loved this feeling! My smaller frame was surrounded by him, his scent wrapping me up as tightly as his arm. Gasoline, evergreen, and sex.

"We all deal with trauma in different ways. I throw myself into the workings of the club. More than once I've taken the heat for Sting and Warlock and risked going back to prison simply because I felt the club would be better served if those men were free to run it. To guide the men of Iron Tzars. The reality was, I wasn't sure I could survive outside of prison in the long term. I still struggle with it sometimes. Before you call bullshit on that, let me tell you that I've spent as much of my life in prison as I've spent out of it. Other than the last six years, only my childhood was spent outside of a cell. I was more comfortable on the inside than I am in polite society."

His confession stunned me for more than one reason. I knew he'd been to prison, but for him to have been in there that long meant he'd likely killed someone. No one got that kind of time outside of tax evasion or some other white-collar shit involving taking money from the federal government, and Brick wasn't that kind of criminal. Unless he'd accrued a shit ton of time while he was incarcerated, but that seemed a bit extreme. No. He'd killed. I could see it in every line of his face. He'd seen death more than once and had sent men to their graves knowing full well what he was doing.

Without my knowledge, my arms wrapped around Brick as far as they could manage. I was stunned when I realized what I'd done but wasn't about to pull away from him. It felt too good. We stood like that for a while, his chin resting on my head, both of us holding each other. I buried my face in his chest and took in more of his scent. His heartbeat was loud in my ear, as was the air moving through his lungs.

Brick gave me one hard squeeze before stepping back. I wanted to throw myself at him but managed to refrain. Barely. Thank goodness he took my hand and tugged me after him.

"Come on, little warrior. Back to bed. We've still got some stuff to clear up between us, and it's getting settled now."

Well, that wasn't ominous or anything.

He led me to the bed and helped me in before following. I tried to move to my side of the bed, but, honestly. With a man his size, there was no my side/his side of the bed. Secondly, Brick snagged me around the waist and pulled me against him, urging me to lie with my head on his shoulder and pinning my hand to his chest underneath his palm.

"Comfortable?"

I wanted to tell him, no, I was very uncomfortable, and could I move to a room of my own, but that was the very last thing I wanted to do. Instead, I nodded, not trusting myself to speak.

"Words, Serelda. Talk to me."

"Yes." My voice came out thready. My heart was pounding. What was he going to tell me? What did he want to get straight between us? Was he about to let me down easy? Tell me he knew I had a crush on him, but he wasn't the man for me? That he'd take me back to Iron Tzars and my sister or to Black Reign and be my protector until then, but I needed to understand he needed a woman not as damaged as me?

"Turn off that brilliant mind of yours, Serelda. All you're doin' is causing yourself pain, and I won't have it. Not when there's no reason for it." His arms tightened around me, and he pulled me even closer to him. Knowing I was hurting, even from my own stupid musings, made him need to protect me from it. That's who Brick was. My protector.

"You can't command me to stop thinking and expect me to comply. It's impossible." I felt compelled to point that out.

"I can in this instance, because there's no need for it."

"You have no idea what I'm thinking," I snapped. Finally, I'd found my backbone. I tried to push away from him, but he didn't budge.

"I'm bettin' it has something to do with that woman you saw me with at the party."

I froze. It was one thing to suspect he knew how I felt about him. Quite another to have those suspicions confirmed.

"That's what I thought, little warrior. Now. You ran from me. You ain't runnin' this time. You're gonna hear me out, and we're gonna move forward. Together."

"What if I don't want to be with you?"

"You do. If you didn't, you wouldn't have gotten upset or been hurt. So we're gonna address some things and clear the air between us. From now on, we talk to each other."

"We don't do a lot of talking," I whispered. "It's mostly you pulling me out of one nightmare or another. Real and imaginary."

He sighed. "There's nothing for you to worry about with the guy on the bus. Sting is making sure it's taken care of, and Wylde has the guy's ID and social security number. He'll find out everything there is to know about the bastard. Then we'll work on finding the man he said he was taking you to."

"Let's get this over with, Brick. I can't take much more without some alone time."

"Stop it." His voice was menacing as he frowned down at me. "You're never going to be alone again. You have me. You have your sister. If you need them, you have the ol' ladies and other friends you made at Black Reign. Much as I hate to throw it out there, you've even got that bastard Rycks if you need him. But I plan on making it so you only need me and your sister until you make more friends at Iron Tzars. Get me?"

I froze, not wanting to read more into his words than were really there. "No. I don't understand."

"Then I'll spell it out for you. We're together. You and me. I'm yours. You're mine."

I shook my head, jerking like he'd slapped me. "You're lying!" I spat the words at him, shoving away but not getting far. Brick held me in a vise-like grip, keeping me firmly against him. The infuriating bastard didn't even grunt.

"Am not. Want me to explain?"

"The woman with you at that party was explanation enough!"

"Serelda, I didn't think you wanted a man in your life. Especially not one like me." He plowed on like I hadn't even spoken. "Not like that anyway. I knew you had your uses for me, but you'd even told me straight out you had no intention of ever letting a man touch you again. I knew you cared for me. I was your protector, and someone you felt safe with. Probably because I'm a big bastard and made you feel like I'd keep anyone and everyone away from you." He had a point. "But somewhere in there, over those last few weeks, I started to feel more for you. There was no way I was going to let you find that out and push me away out of fear. So I felt sorry for myself and got drunk. When I got drunk, I let my guard down around the club girls. I hadn't been with any of them in a while. Longer than normal. One of them approached me. I might have flirted with her out of habit, but I didn't want her or any other woman. Honestly, Serelda. I was so drunk that night, there was no way anything was happening anyway. And you have no idea how much it pains me to tell you that."

I lay still against Brick, not even wanting to breathe as I considered his words. Did I believe him? Did it matter? Yes. It mattered. As to whether I believed him, I wasn't sure. I wanted to believe him, but nothing seemed to make sense to me.

"I don't -- I don't under -- understand." Try as I might, my voice broke. I was so near shattering it wasn't even funny. Brick was right. He was my safe place. The one person I knew was capable of keeping me safe no matter what, even more so than my sister. Had he not come for me when I'd run? Killed for me when I'd been in danger? Sure, other people had been affected, but I knew the second I told Brick the man had a knife on me, Brick would kill the bastard.

Brick took a breath, seeming unsure exactly what he was going to do. Then he pulled me fully on top of him so I straddled his hips. I gasped, bracing myself on his wide chest. When I would have pushed off him, he wrapped those muscled arms around me and melted away any resistance.

"From this point forward, Serelda, we're a team. You and me. Not only that, but I'm gonna coax you into accepting my body. You're gonna be mine in every way you can. I'm already yours. You have to be brave enough, trusting enough, to take me."

My heart pounded and sweat erupted over my skin. "You... you *want* me?"

His brows drew together. "I do. That so hard to

believe?"

I felt tears form in my eyes. Watched in horror as one dripped from my face onto his lips. Brick's tongue darted out to capture the moisture, and my breath hitched. My heart pounded. *I wanted this*! Wanted Brick with everything in my being.

"But… my face…"

"Is beautiful. It's the face of a warrior. You think I'd accept anything less than a warrior for my woman?"

"I'm not a warrior, Brick. I think you know that."

He tucked a strand of my hair behind my ear. "Don't think so? So it was someone else who dropped my ass with a Taser, then, hmm? What about that woman who sat there while some fuck had a knife in her side? I saw him dig you with it. You didn't flinch once. You could have been sitting on a fuckin' couch having fuckin' tea with the King of England for all the pain you showed. I've never met a woman who was your equal. Even your sister. *You*, Serelda. *You*. Are exactly what I want. Exactly what I need."

Before I could form a reply, Brick curled his fingers around my neck and pulled me down gently for a kiss. His hand moved from my neck to my cheek as he brushed his lips gently over mine. I gasped, and he flicked his tongue against mine before breaking the contact.

I cried out before diving back to him. I was afraid I'd mashed something, but Brick chuckled. He allowed me to deepen the kiss, letting me explore with my tongue before thrusting his own back into my mouth once more.

Kissing Brick was the sweetest euphoria. Never had I imagined a man's lips could feel this good on mine. He held me close without pinning me. At least, it didn't feel like I was pinned. In fact, I wanted to be closer to him. My arms went around his neck, and I tried to kiss him so he'd know this was what I wanted. When he grunted at me, his hand sliding back to bunch in my hair, I was pretty sure he got the message.

"Little warrior." His gruff, deep voice sent shivers through me. "You like kissin' me?"

"Yes." My answer was a breathy whimper.

"Like me kissin' you?"

"You know I do."

"Do you have any fuckin' idea how long I've wanted to have you like this? In my arms. In my bed. Understand me, Serelda. This is where you're gonna stay."

Then he took my mouth again. I loved the way his muscled arms bunched around me. Most especially, I loved our size differences. I was aware of how tiny I was wrapped in arms that went all the way around me. The fact that he was wound so tightly around me and didn't make me panic was a miracle, but then, since the first day I'd met him, Brick had been different. Something inside me called to him, wanting to find a home within his arms when I never wanted to be near a man in any kind of intimate situation ever again. Brick had changed *everything*.

With one hard squeeze, Brick let me go, sliding his hands down my body to my ass, cupping and squeezing my cheeks. Animalistic growls came from his throat as he continued to kiss me, flicking his tongue against mine over and over. Thoroughly tasting me, giving me time to adjust to the new sensations. The man was as careful as he could be, all the while stoking the fire inside me to a conflagration I had no hope of controlling.

His hand slipped down into the waistband of my

pants to find my flesh. The defeated groan that came from him then was nearly my undoing.

"God! How the fuck are you so fuckin' perfect, Serelda? I can't wait to fuck you from behind. I bet this --" he squeezed one cheek of my ass hard before relaxing his grip "-- will jiggle every time my cock pushes into your pussy. Bet it'll make me want to pull out and come on it. Mark it as mine. Like every single part of you is mine."

"Brick!" I shuddered, feeling my pussy let loose a rush of moisture as he expressed his desire. "Oh, God!" I felt his cock between our bodies and shifted so that he was nestled between my pussy lips through my pants. My thin panties and leggings had no hope of keeping him out. Thank God, because once I was settled over him the way I wanted, the pressure on my clit gave me a hint at what I'd been missing in life. What had been stolen from me by sadistic men who didn't deserve even one more thought from me. I knew it would take more than one simple epiphany in the middle of such a passionate encounter, but it was something I was determined to overcome. Especially if the man who held me so protectively, gently, and fiercely was the man to help me slay my demons. Brick.

It took me a second, but I finally figured out how to move to get the friction I needed. My breath came in shallow pants, and my hips snapped up and down in an erratic movement. My keening cries were swallowed by Brick's kiss even as he encouraged me to keep going.

"That's it, little warrior. Take what you need. "

"I don't know what I need! Help me!"

"You got this, baby. Keep movin' on me. Feels so fuckin' good. Gonna come with you. You take the lead."

"Brick!" I screamed in a panic, his husky voice and dirty talk finally pushing me over the edge. It was the first time in my life I'd orgasmed. The sensations were at once exhilarating and terrifying. My eyes were wide-open looking into Brick's. I knew he saw the shock on my face, because his eyes widened and his lips parted before he got a determined look on his face and his hands tightened on my hips.

"Fuck! Don't stop. Ride it out."

I did as he instructed. His cock pulsed against my clit, and it triggered another burst of pleasure. Again, I screamed. This time, Brick wrapped his arms back around me and thrust upward, his cock throbbing like mad. He groaned loudly, his body shuddering under mine. I felt warm liquid between us and knew he'd come as well. Both of us breathed heavily. Sweat dampened both of us.

Brick ran one big hand up and down my back while the other arm was wrapped solidly around me, holding me to him.

"You good, little warrior?"

"I don't know. Maybe?"

He barked out a laugh. "OK. Yeah. I get it. But did I scare you? Did I hurt you?"

"What?" I lifted myself up to look at him. I knew my eyes were wide as I looked at him, not believing the question. "I can't believe you'd ask that! NO! You did *not* hurt me or scare me." I raised a hand to brush over his beard, reveling in the ability to do so. Because he was mine. "That was the most wonderful thing I've ever experienced."

"It went further than I'd intended, but if you're good with it, I don't regret it." He leaned up and gave me a lingering kiss. Then he sat up, taking me with him when he stood. I wrapped my legs around him as he carried me to the bathroom. "Need to clean us up. Afraid I made a mess."

I couldn't help the giggle that burst free. "I think we both did."

He glanced down, stepping back a little. Sure enough, there was a large wet spot over my crotch. I should probably be mortified. Though I'd never experienced this kind of pleasure, I wasn't ignorant of how things worked. I'd felt the moisture expelled from my pussy. Knew it had been something I couldn't control so I tried not to be embarrassed about it. I'd have to change my clothes, though.

Brick got a smug, contented look on his face. "So we did. Get undressed, and I'll clean you up. Then we'll grab some sleep before heading home tomorrow. My brothers are coming as escorts, given the problems we had. Not expectin' trouble, but I'll feel better with some backup."

The reminder of trouble should have put a damper on the mood, but I was so happy nothing could bring me down. At least, not right now. And not with Brick solidly in my corner.

Chapter Four
Serelda

I watched as he stripped, letting me see his muscled, tattooed body in full. He wasn't shy about it, stripping off without hesitation. He was covered in ink. Most of it was prison ink, but there were a few I saw now that were beautifully done. Most of them had something to do with Iron Tzars.

Absently, I slid from my perch on the sink and reached out to trace a tattoo on his shoulder. One elbow had a spider web around it. There was a pocket watch with a long, winding chain at his hip and around his back. I wasn't well versed in gang tattoos, but I didn't see anything that jumped out at me. Nothing indicating he'd been affiliated with white supremacists.

"They're a mix."

My gaze shot up to his face. He watched me carefully. "What?"

"My tats."

"Oh. Yes. Prison and artistic."

He nodded. "You won't find any gang affiliations. It was hard, and I took beatings for it, but I stayed out of them. It was more because I was determined to take my punishment like a man. If that meant I got the shit beat out of me, I'd take it on my own. As time went on and I survived, I was glad I hadn't given in and joined a gang for protection. I did my time, then got out. I have no loyalties to anyone other than Sting and the Iron Tzars."

"What about Warlock?"

He seemed to think about that one before nodding. "To an extent. By all rights, I should have had to kill him. He betrayed the club, which is punishable by death. I can't go into everything, but Iron Tzars is… hard core, I guess you could say. No one leaves the club. The only reason Warlock did was because El Diablo demanded he come to Black Reign."

"El Diablo gets what he wants." I knew this well. Had seen it on many occasions from the shadows.

"He's more than he seems. Which I'm sure you know." He smiled down at me, then pulled off my shirt and knelt in front of me, sliding my pants and panties from my hips and down my legs. Taking a wet cloth, he gently cleaned my belly, my inner thighs, and between my legs. Once done, he wiped it over himself before tossing the cloth in the corner. He kissed my hip bone before standing. "Warlock gave me a chance with the Tzars, but only because Sting vouched for me. So, to answer your question, I feel like I owe Warlock, but I'm only loyal to Sting. I'd defend that man with my life. Same as I would you."

We stood there, staring at each other. I realized now that Brick had done this on purpose. He wanted me to see his body and the marks of his prison life so I'd let him see my body and all its scars.

He reached out and traced one long, raised mark along the curve of my breast on the side. That one had been particularly deep. I remembered when my tormentor had given it to me. The man I now knew was named the Cannibal. That is, assuming the guy from the bus was right and I was indeed marked. Through all the cuts they'd put on my body, it was hard to imagine anyone could pick out two and know who'd done this to me. Something inside me, though, told me this was the real deal.

"I want you to understand that I will find the motherfucker who did this to you, and I'm going to kill him." He met my gaze. "I don't say that lightly, or ever in a place with questionable security. But I'm tellin' you now. It doesn't matter who knows or what the consequences are for me. I'm going to capture him. Mark his body exactly like he marked you. Then I'm going to make him suffer for days. Weeks. When he finally starts to heal, I'm gonna slice him open again. Over and over until this rage inside me has been satisfied."

"You look intense, but not enraged." I reached up and traced the line over his brow. His eyes slid shut as if the mere touch of my skin on his was a soothing balm to his every woe.

"Because havin' you with me soothes my need to kill. When I find him, you're not gonna be anywhere near that fucker."

I shook my head. "Not happening, Brick." I dropped my hand and gave him my fiercest glare. "When we find the son of a bitch, vengeance is mine. And no one else's other than Winter's. We earned that right, and no one is taking it away from us."

Brick jerked like I'd struck him. Then I glanced down. His cock, which had only been semi hard, shot up hard and proud, the tip leaking precum.

"Now, there you went. I'm lovin' this bloodthirsty side of you. At least, when you don't tase me."

"Get used to it. I'm done being a victim. I'm taking back my life because you deserve a strong woman at your side. Not someone weak and beaten down. I came with Winter to Indiana to start a new life. It's time I got to it."

"There's my warrior woman." He lifted his chin, grinning down at me. "Knew she was in there." Brick pulled me to him and kissed me with a sweeping thrust of his tongue. "When we get home, I'm gonna take you as far as you'll let me. I'll push you outside your comfort zone, but I swear, I'll never push too far."

I blinked up at him. "Brick, there is nowhere I wouldn't follow you. Only you. Where you lead us, I'll follow willingly and trust you'll take care of me. And so you know, I'm ready now. There's no reason to wait."

"Fuck…" Brick scrubbed a hand over his mouth, smoothing his beard down his chin as he went. "You're gonna make one fine ol' lady to the VP of Iron Tzars. I'll have the fiercest, bravest woman in that whole Goddamn compound, and I will flaunt that fact every chance I get." When I took his hand and placed it on my breast, he shivered and squeezed gently. "Not here, baby. The first time I fuck you is gonna be in my own fuckin' bed. We might not leave it for days, but I'm gonna wait until I have you home if it fuckin' kills me. You deserve that respect."

I wanted to protest, but I could tell by the state of his arousal it was a big concession for him. One he demanded of himself. His cock was angry, the head purple. One pearly drop glistened from the head, and I couldn't resist. I sank to my knees in front of him. Before he could stop me, I engulfed his cock with my mouth, sinking down as far as I comfortably could.

"Christ! Serelda! Fuck!" Brick's hands both shot to my head, tunneling through my hair and gripping hard. He gave a sharp grunt and rewarded me with another drop of that tantalizing fluid. I wanted to swallow him down. Wanted to give him as much pleasure as he'd given me. Sure, he'd come with me, but I wanted more for him.

I hummed as I took him deeper. The way his thighs quivered where I rested my palms on them to balance myself gave me courage to continue. Looking up at the massive man, I let his cock slide free before taking him again. And again. Brick's jaw tightened, and his cock throbbed in my mouth.

"You better fuckin' pull back if you don't want my load down your throat, girl." I narrowed my eyes at him, daring him to take away my treat. "All right, then. Get ready."

Seconds later, he threw his head back and roared. Hot seed shot into my mouth and down my throat. I swallowed what I could, but I knew some leaked from the corner of my mouth, dripping down my chin to land on my bare chest.

I floated. The feeling surrounding me was one of euphoria. Like a drug. I was flying on the pleasure I'd given Brick, and I didn't ever want to come down. Brick's hand bunched in my hair as he wiped my face with a warm towel, his touch serving to ground me when the high I'd flown to threatened to take me away. I'd done this on my own. Brick hadn't suggested it or coaxed me into it. This was all me. It had been the most freeing experience of my life! His pleasure was all mine. I'd given him something I hoped he would always remember, since I knew I'd never forget.

Finally, he let go of my hair, bending to pick me up by my arms, and pulled me against him into his embrace. "Goddamn, woman. What the fuck did you do to me?"

"Did... did I do wrong?" If he hadn't enjoyed that, I doubted I'd recover. I'd just had the best feeling of my life, had been nearly drunk on the adrenaline coursing through my veins as I'd watched him shout to the ceiling when he came down my throat.

"What?" He barked the question at me before shaking his head fiercely. "No! Of course not! I've never experienced anything like that in my life!"

Relief was so strong, if Brick hadn't been holding me, I'd have collapsed into a heap. "Good," I managed to get out. "That's good."

Brick swung me up into his arms, carrying me to the bed. "You're trying my patience, woman. I am not gonna fuck you in a cheap motel for our first time together." He shook his head as if to clear it. "Abso-*fuckin'*-lutely not!"

I clung to him, not wanting him to let me go. He didn't. Instead, he climbed into the bed with me held tightly against him. Somehow he got the covers over us and the light switched out. I lay with my head on his shoulder and my hand on his wide chest. The high I'd felt earlier now left me drained, but pleasantly so.

"Mine," I said as I settled against him, knowing sleep wasn't going to be long in claiming me.

"Yeah, baby. I'm all yours."

"I'm yours too, Brick."

"Damned straight." He kissed my forehead. "Sleep. Got a long ride ahead of us tomorrow. Once I talk with Wylde and Sting and figure out our next move, we're gonna have an even longer night. Want you rested so I can wear you out."

With a happy sigh, I mumbled something I hoped made sense. Probably didn't. Because I fell into the deepest, most restful sleep I'd had in longer than I could remember.

***

Brick

I let Serelda sleep in the next morning. I'd kept her up half the night learning her body and letting her explore mine. And, Lord, she was eager to learn every single thing she could about how to drive me fucking crazy. My little warrior woke me with her mouth working my cock and refused to stop until I'd come down her throat again. When I did, I pulled her over me to straddle my face while I ate her until she did the same. That had been something she'd resisted at first, but only because she was afraid she'd smother me. Honestly, I wouldn't have cared if she did. Once I had a taste of her, I knew it was going to be one of my favorite things to do.

Sting had sent Atlas, Blaze, Eagle, and Shooter to escort us back. Shooter and Atlas were in a Bronco while the other men were on bikes. It made for eyes in front and back as well as giving Shooter the ability to guard us and take out anyone threatening us. I didn't expect trouble, but we were ready for it. Hopefully, we'd be ready to leave in a couple of hours.

"Brick?"

"Right here, little warrior. Gettin' things ready to leave. You good?" I sat down beside her and brushed an unruly lock of hair off her cheek.

She graced me with a sleepy smile. "Yeah. Little tired, though I slept wonderfully. You know. When you let me sleep."

I chuckled. "You were as guilty as me, and I ain't complainin'."

"Never said I minded." She reached up to hook her arms around my neck and pull me down for a kiss. "You gave me the most wonderful night of my life, Brick. I look forward to more when we get back home. I'm sorry I ran from you. I just couldn't stand the thought of…" Her breath hitched, and she trailed off, her brows knitting together in distress.

"Of me being with someone else?"

She shook her head violently. "Of you pitying me. That you were only with me, helping me, because you felt sorry for me. I wanted you to want me too."

"I do, baby. I didn't realize you were ready for a more physical relationship and that you'd chosen me." I leaned in to kiss her again. "Kinda thought you only wanted me because I made you feel safe. I was willing to settle for that if it meant I got to be with you."

"Then why did you go to that party?" She looked so hurt it nearly gutted me. This was the woman so self-conscious of her scars she was painfully shy. I never wanted her to retreat to that version of herself. She was so strong and resilient, she deserved to have the world at her feet. Not to feel like she needed to hide from it.

"Good Goddamn question." I sighed. "My brothers were razzin' me for following you around like a lost puppy when you weren't in any way interested in me. I was never going to that party to find a woman. I wanted to get drunk and feel sorry for myself for the first time in my life." I scowled at her, trying to lighten the mood. "That's what you reduced me to, woman. Twenty-five years in prison and I never once looked back. A few weeks in your company, holdin' you, comfortin' you without being able to kiss you? Yeah. I had a fuckin' pity party."

As I'd hoped, she smiled. She reached up and stroked my beard. "Can I ask you a question?"

"Anything, honey. Ask all you want. I'll never lie to you."

"Why did you go to prison?"

I knew this question was coming. I didn't dread it exactly. I hated admitting my failures to her. "I was driving impaired and killed a man. Didn't matter that it was an accident, I made a choice. I got behind the wheel knowing I shouldn't." She made a sound of distress and gripped my hand tightly. "I was in the Marines. Had just passed my SEAL training, which was the reason for the celebration. Everyone at that fuckin' party was drunk, but I was the one who chose to drive everyone home."

"What happened?"

I shrugged. "We were all talking. Laughing. Raisin' hell, I guess. I looked back over my shoulder to say something to my buddy. Ran a red. We got hit in the side, and my brother sitting in the back passenger seat took the brunt of the impact. He was dead before the fuckin' car stopped."

"Oh, no!"

I squeezed her hand. "Anyway. I passed all the reflex tests and whatnot, but then they had me do a breathalyzer, and I was over the limit, if barely."

"If you were in control, why did they give you so much time?"

"One drink is too many drinks, baby. You know that."

"It seems unfair. I mean, that could have happened to anyone." The empathy in her voice made me smile. She was such a sweet thing. Until someone crossed her. The pricks in my chest where her Taser had hit its mark still stung.

"I knew better. The man who died was the son of an admiral so instead of charging me with a lesser charge of involuntary manslaughter, they went for the maximum they thought they could make stick. Voluntary manslaughter, meaning the act had been deliberate. And, honestly, I couldn't argue with them. While my intent may not have been to kill anyone, like in the heat of the moment, I'd made a conscious decision to drink and then get behind the wheel of a vehicle." I waved a hand as if it all didn't matter. "Anyway, they took it to the judge with a bunch of other charges, and I plead guilty. Because I was."

She gasped. "Brick! You did what?"

"Honey, I was completely in the wrong. My appointed JAG tried to get me to let him work out a plea, but I refused. I plead guilty and took my punishment like a man. With all the secondary charges and whatnot, I got ten additional years on top of the fifteen for the manslaughter charge, and since the admiral had pull, they ran the sentences consecutively instead of concurrently."

"That doesn't seem fair. And I thought you only had to serve part of a sentence. Like half or something."

"Sometimes, but you have to have good behavior and various other things. Remember me telling you I refused to join the gangs?"

"Yeah."

"That meant I fought. A lot. Killed more than once in self-defense. While they didn't increase my time, saying I had no choice, it impacted my parole hearings. I suspect the admiral had something to do with that, too. I knew it would and never contested any hearing. I did the crime. I'd do my time. And I did."

"I don't know of anyone who would have done that, Brick."

"Don't look at me like I made some kind of noble sacrifice. I got my friend killed. I deserved exactly what I got and more. When I got out, I was in a pretty bad way. Overwhelmed, I guess you could say. That's when I met Sting. I'd gotten in a fight with six gang members who'd been told to take me out. One of the men I'd killed on the inside had been affiliated with them.

"They were beatin' the shit out of me. I was fightin' back, but six on one, no matter how big I am, was more than I could defend against. Then this little prick got involved. Sting was twenty-three and so fuckin' cocky I wanted to smack him upside the head." I chuckled, remembering the man I now protected with my life. "He jumped in the fight, running his mouth and nearly got the shit beat out of him, too. Seein' the kid who came to my defense in trouble gave me the extra something I needed to finish the fight. Two of those motherfuckers died. The other four ran. Obviously, they weren't going to the police, so we had time to decide what to do. Sting called Warlock, and the Iron Tzars disposed of the bodies. Sting wanted me brought into the fold, but Warlock wasn't a dumbass. He did give me a chance, though. Let me prove myself before they made me a prospect, then I spent another year provin' I was a good fit for the Tzars."

"Is that why you're so loyal to Sting?"

"Yeah. He had no idea who I was or what I'd done, but he came to my defense. He said it was because he saw the tattoo on my forearm." I extended my arm and let her see the special forces tattoo I'd had done the night my life went to hell. "He said that, no matter what had happened in my life after, I'd served my country and passed tests few people in the world could pass. I took him under my wing and helped him learn to control his temper. He earned his rank within the Iron Tzars and brought me up with him. We have each other's back. No matter what."

"I'm glad. If he hadn't come to your defense, I'd never have met you."

"We did meet, Serelda. And we ain't ever gonna be apart. You get me?"

She smiled. God, would I ever get tired of seeing that beautiful smile? "I get you, Brick."

"Xander."

"What?"

"My name. Xander Scott."

"Is that what you want me to call you? Because I'm not sure I can. You're Brick. The wall between me and everyone else."

"Which I love." I brought her hand to my lips and kissed her palm. "You can call me whatever you like. Just thought you should know my name since you're my ol' lady. You'll have your patch soon as we get back to Iron Tzars."

She looked shocked, like she hadn't expected that. "What?"

"You heard me, baby. I had your patch made weeks ago. Same time I got Sting Winter's patch. Just wasn't sure when I'd be able to give it to you." Tears filled her eyes even as she smiled. "You didn't think I was serious?"

"No!" She laughed. "It's not that. I… I guess the thought of getting a biker's property patch has come to mean more to me than I'd realized."

"Told you, honey. I'm yours. You're mine."

"Yes. Agreed."

"I don't think Sting's approached Winter yet, and I almost hate to tell you, but the second all this becomes official, I've got to get you inked."

"Inked? Like a tattoo?"

"Yeah. It will say 'Property of Brick,' like your vest. It's another layer of protection for you, but also reinforces to you what you've signed up for."

"Is there something I need to know?" She didn't look scared or worried, just curious.

"I'll tell you when we get home. It's not something we talk about outside the compound. It won't matter anyway, because I'll keep you happy. I swear it."

Yeah. There was definitely something she needed

to know. Like no one leaves Iron Tzars. It's one of the reasons so few of us had ol' ladies. Warlock broke with tradition when he took on Beverly. In the end, he'd had to kill her, but it had only reinforced the fact that we had to keep to the rules originally set by the club when it was founded in the forties, right after World War Two.

That would have to come later. Telling the women would be hard enough, and I had no idea how either of them would react. It was something Sting and I needed to discuss. Very soon.

Chapter Five
Brick

We rolled into the Iron Tzars compound at two in the afternoon. Winter met us the second the vehicle stopped. She jerked open the door to Serelda's side and wrapped her sister in a fierce hug.

"Don't you ever leave me again! You hear me?" She sounded angry as hell but clung to Serelda so hard I thought I was going to have to break it up.

"I won't, Winter. I'm so sorry."

"Why? What made you run?"

"Stupidity and jealousy. I'm good now." Serelda actually laughed as she said it. "But only because I'm going to be Brick's ol' lady."

"*What*?"

"No, you're not," I said, scowling down at Serelda. "You're not *gonna* be anything. You *are* my ol' lady. As in right now this fuckin' minute. I just gotta give you the patch." I glanced up at Sting and Roman. Both men had come to greet us, and I knew Roman would never be far away from Winter. Like I'd never again be far from Serelda. "And stuff," I added. When Roman winced, I knew he hadn't broached the topic with Winter either. The girls giggled and continued to hug each other, completely ignoring me.

Roman stepped toward me, gripping my shoulder in support. "We gonna do this?"

"Got to," I said. "After what happened with Bev and Warlock, we have to set the example. Tzars for life."

"And the kids?"

That was something I hadn't thought of, but I was sure it had been taken into account. "We'll figure it out. Obviously, we'll have to be careful. Set boundaries for them. Areas they are not allowed into for any reason. I ain't inkin' a kid, though. And if they want a different life, they should be able to have it. It's not like they had much choice in the matter. Unlike our women."

"We'll work it out." Sting sounded confident. The kid was smart. I had no doubt he already had something he was working on in his head. He needed time to pull it together, then he'd run it by me and we'd perfect it together. It's what we did.

"Any word on that Cannibal character? That little shit from the bus was the only person to approach the women since Black Reign took them in. You think he was tellin' the truth or feedin' her some line of bullshit?"

"Oh, he wasn't lyin'." Wylde, our intel officer, came up behind me. I reached for his hand in greeting, pulling him in for a quick clap on the back. "The shit Rayburn Mills was into back in the day preceded dark web shit. They did their business through mediators or hacked satellite feeds. Cyber security wasn't what it is today. Anything controlled in a network was vulnerable if you knew what you were doing. What I found I got through facial recognition. This Cannibal guy likes to brag about his work." He glanced to where the women were having their reunion, then motioned for us to step farther away. "I found posts for both women when they were in the Cannibal's possession. He filmed everything he did. The rapes. The torture. All of it. It's now on a website where he shows off what he does. There are, literally, hundreds of women and older girls. Most of them didn't seem to survive, from what I can tell. Winter and Serelda, though… They're his 'masterpieces.'" He made air quotes. "He got word of your handiwork, Brick. With the guy you sent me the info on. Now, he's put out a hit on you, and a capture reward for the women."

"Both of them?" I crossed my arms over my chest, trying to calm myself when all I wanted to do was take Serelda away and hide in the mountains somewhere even God wouldn't find her. Which was stupid. The club compound was the safest place she could be. On the off chance someone tracked us here, there were dozens of brothers to protect her. Not only me.

"Yeah." Wylde scrubbed a hand over the back of his neck. "I know a fuckin' tattoo won't do much to warn that bastard away from them but having them inked would go a long way toward the rest of the club accepting them. That's part of the reason no one accepted Bev like they normally would have. Which was why she didn't do more damage than she did. We all knew that, as long as Warlock didn't ink her, he didn't completely trust her. So, you guys need to figure out what to do. Given their history, I can see how it might be difficult. But you know it's what needs to be done."

"Fully aware, brother. I'd hoped to wait until all three had settled in, but that may not be possible." Roman gave me a hard look, obviously feeling the same way I did. "Safety trumps comfort. This has to be done. Today."

"Iris needs hers, too. Might as well do all three women together." Sting wasn't about to let us force our women into doing something he wasn't willing to subject his own woman to. "I'd hoped to give her time to think about it, but you're right. This has become a safety issue."

"Ace should be back this evening. I'll let him know he has work." Wylde left me, Sting, and Roman.

I glanced toward the woman.

"No reason to think they'd be opposed," Roman said with a shrug.

"No reason to think they won't see us as the ones scarring them this time. Only instead of knife wounds, we're forcing them to get a tattoo. With 'Property of' permanently written on their skin." The more I thought about it the more I hated it. I wanted her to wear my ink, but I absolutely would not allow her to put me in the same category with the beasts who brutalized her years ago. I *was* a beast. But I was *her* beast. I'd fight and kill for her.

"You know we have to do this, Brick. If not, we need to send them back to Black Reign now, and I for one am not willing to do that. Winter's my woman. I never want to be without her."

"I know, brother. Doesn't mean I have to like it."

"I never really thought about this where it concerned Winter. Should have. That's on me." Roman rubbed his chin, stroking his beard. "I have my own ink, as do you. It's part of being in this MC. In most MCs."

"Most MCs don't ask this of their women, though. I suppose some do, but the Tzars have had hard and fast rules for longer than either of us has been alive. The ol' ladies might as well be patched members. We hold them to the same standard."

"Yeah. No divorce. No leaving. If we want to keep our secrets, this is how we have to do things. We might keep club secrets from them, but if you're with someone long enough, you confide in them. Already I see the appeal of having someone to talk with. It's usually you, but…"

"I know. It's different."

"Maybe if they all do it together, side by side, it

will seem less like a punishment." Roman had a point, but I wasn't sure that would be enough.

"If she's gettin' inked, then so am I." I hadn't gotten ink since I got out of prison except my own Iron Tzars brand. It had been forced on me as a way of life on the inside, and I never wanted to be part of that lifestyle again. I'd chosen to be part of Tzars knowing I'd have to be branded because it was a life decision. I was my own man but made stronger for my loyalty to the club. For Serelda, though, I'd do whatever I had to for her to be secure in our relationship. This might be something I could give her to ease any fear she might have regarding her own tattoo as well as her place in my life.

Sting raised an eyebrow. "Yeah? What'er you gonna get?"

I thought for a minute. "I'll get a ring tattoo. Her name on my left-hand ring finger."

"I could get behind that. If Winter can wear my name on her skin, I can do the same for her."

"Makes sense." Sting nodded. "I'm on board, too."

That made me feel more comfortable about the situation, though not totally at peace with it. If she truly balked, I'd figure something else out.

"Don't borrow trouble, brother," Sting said, gripping my shoulder. "They're both stronger than anyone has given them credit for."

"I know. I don't know if I can stand the look in her eyes if she can't do this."

"She can. All three of them can."

The women approached us, arms around each other and huge smiles on their faces. My heart softened even more. It struck me how much I'd fallen for Serelda in such a short time. I'd been drawn to her from the very first, when the sisters had poked their heads up from the back of Sting's Bronco on the way back home from Florida after helping Warlock's woman find her sister. Serelda had hidden behind her sister, obviously terrified of her situation, so at odds with the woman who'd spent the night in my arms last night. I was eager to complete our union, but I knew this had to be settled sooner rather than later.

"Serelda told me you're with her now." Winter smiled up at me. While her smile was bright, to me it was nothing like the one Serelda bestowed on me.

"She did, did she? You good with that?"

Winter rolled her eyes. "Like it matters. You're just like the men from Black Reign. Once you make up your mind you want a woman, you have her." She smiled brightly. "You need to know, though, if you break her heart, I will cut yours out."

Sting burst out laughing. I shook my head, chuckling as I reached out a hand for Serelda. She came to me willingly, wrapping her arms around my middle and snuggling into my chest. "Noted. You can put away your rusty knives, though. I have no intention of ever hurting Serelda. What I *will* do is protect her with my life. Always."

"Good. So. Since we're all here, you know, together. Why don't you give us the bad news."

Roman met my gaze. "What can I say? My woman knows me."

"It's not exactly bad news. Just something we should have told you before we brought you into this world."

"We've been with an MC for a long time, guys." Winter narrowed her eyes as she looked up at Sting. He reached out and tucked an errant curl behind her ear, the breeze tugging it loose again. "What's different about our lives here than when we were in Black Reign?"

"Well, for starters," Sting said, "we ain't got the fancy accommodations. Until we can get some things remodeled, it's pretty basic around here."

"No one said we needed fancy." Serelda looked up at me, and I could see dread in her eyes. She knew there was something coming, and she was afraid. But she didn't pull away. Instead, she clung tighter, her fists bunching in my vest at my back. "What's going on?"

"Let's go inside." I leaned down to kiss Serelda lightly. "We'll sit down and explain everything."

She nodded, looking back at her sister. Winter frowned at Roman but said nothing. Once inside, Sting ushered everyone into his office. Roman sat on the couch and pulled Winter onto his lap. I did the same with Serelda on the love seat.

"Spill it, Sting." Winter tried to get off Roman's lap, but he turned her so she straddled him.

"Calm the hell down, woman." Roman didn't sound irritated or angry. "Waiting for Iris to join us is all."

"So, this has to do with the women." Serelda tucked her legs up so she was curled against me. "Me, Winter, and Iris."

"Yes." Sting nodded. "It's something we should have explained before, but with the events of the last few weeks, it kind of fell to the side."

Iris entered the room. "What's going on?" She smiled in greeting, but I could tell she suspected there was trouble.

"Shut the door, honey." Sting held out a hand to his woman, and Iris did as he asked, then went to him. Sting pulled her into his lap like me and Roman had done. "I'm sorry, baby. We've got trouble coming, and we need to make preparations."

"This is because of what happened on the bus. Isn't it?" Serelda's voice was small as she looked up at me. "I'm sorry, Brick. I never meant to cause trouble."

"You didn't, Tinkerbell. None of that was your fault."

"But if I hadn't run --" I cut her off with a kiss.

"One thing had nothing to do with the other. You heard what the guy said. You've had people watching you for years. That was the first opportunity they'd had in over a decade to catch you by yourself. You've either had someone from Black Reign with you when you left their compound, or you stayed inside. I'm surprised it took someone this long to make a try for you."

"Roman filled me in on some of what happened, but I get the feeling there are things we don't know." Winter was entering hellcat mode. I could see the cocky smirk on Roman's face. The man loved his hellcat as much as I loved my warrior.

"Sting, what's going on?" Iris looked like she suspected a trap. She'd be right.

"Winter and Serelda have someone after them. Turns out, the man who hurt them years ago wants them back." Winter's jaw tightened, but she stayed silent. Serelda whimpered a little but otherwise stayed quiet. "He's called the Cannibal. Not a lot on him, but Wylde says our girls here are two of the very few who survived him. Since they escaped, he's fixated on them. Didn't take too kindly to Brick killin' the man he sent after them. So Brick has a bounty on his head, and the two of you have a reward offered for your return to the bastard."

Winter stuck her chin up. "I see him again, I'm

killin' him." She didn't look afraid. She looked supremely pissed. I believed every word she said. "Set up a meeting with him. Tell him you're bringing us to him. I'll take care of the rest."

"Not happenin'."

"The fuck we will."

"Are you out of your fuckin' mind?"

All three of us spoke on top of each other.

"No fuckin' way, Winter." Roman shook his head and pulled his woman closer. "Not in a million years will I allow that."

"You can't allow me anything, Roman. I'm my own person. We brought this to your door. We'll take care of our own mess."

"That's exactly what we're here to discuss. And by discuss, I mean you're going to do what the president of this fuckin' club tells you." I winced. Sting was in full president mode. He hadn't yet learned to tone it down around the women. When it came to making hard decisions for the club, though, there was no give in him. The fact that his own woman could be in danger made the situation worse for him. Asking him to rein it in wouldn't have been the smart way to calm him down.

"I know you didn't just say that." Iris narrowed her eyes at Sting. "We're not members of this club, Sting. And I can promise you, you'll catch more flies with honey than you will with vinegar. Don't pull rank on me. It will always bite you in the ass."

Roman barked out a laugh. I buried my face in my woman's neck, shamelessly hiding my own smile. The girls were silent, none of them looking as amused as me and Roman.

Sting closed his eyes and took a deep, calming breath. "How about I start over."

"Seems like a sound decision." Iris was one damned fine ol' lady for our president.

"You know the problems Warlock had before he left Iron Tzars. Right?"

"Yes. You told me about Warlock's ex and what happened."

"Right. Warlock, my dad, took up with a woman with questionable motives. The short of it is, she was a spy for the CIA. Things aren't as bad with law enforcement and MCs now as it was back in the day, but some of what Iron Tzars does is on the wrong side of the law. Add to that our ties with Argent Tech in Illinois and they really wanted to get an 'in' into the club."

"But Bones and Salvation's Bane both have a close relationship with Argent." Winter had blossomed with Roman. She was becoming as assertive as an enforcer's woman needed to be. "You're not unique in that."

"No. But both Bones and Bane have something else in common we don't."

"ExFil," Serelda said softly. "Rycks says Cain has government contacts through ExFil. Since they're paramilitary and work closely with the CIA, it's unlikely they'd target the hands that protect them out of the country."

"Exactly," Sting said, looking proud that our women understood the subtitles of politics in this situation. "They can't get Argent to agree to give them the more sensitive software, and they can't alienate their biggest, most reliable security contractor. So they chose us."

"Did Warlock know?" Winter asked.

"I think so. Maybe not at first, but he knew. She was his woman, but he never made it official. It was unspoken."

"So no property patch." Again it was Winter who spoke. "What's this got to do with us?"

"You're all getting your vests today."

"Great. Where are they?"

"There's more, baby." Roman brushed her cheek tenderly as he turned her to face him. "This club has been around since right after World War Two. The laws that govern us are there to protect us. From the very beginning we were outlaws. Not in the sense we were into the drugs and sex most MCs were at the time, though there was plenty of that. Back then, the Tzars were Nazi hunters when the war ended. Tried to round up as many as they could before they could escape Europe and scatter to the winds. Most of the original Tzars fought in Europe and saw the carnage firsthand. When they decided to take matters into their own hands, they did all of it underground. No one sanctioned it. They knew that getting international justice would never be possible, no matter what kind of trial the rest of the world put on. So they hunted and killed hundreds of the bastards. No trials. Nothing sanctioned. The only people they worked with were a few of the newly formed Mossad in Israel. And that was four or five years after the war."

"After that, we expanded to hunting terrorists and, more recently, human traffickers. That's been our primary objective for the last twenty years or so." Sting took up the narrative. "Needless to say, there were times various organizations tried to infiltrate us. Some of them domestic. Some foreign. Other clubs who trafficked. Other branches of the government whose interests weren't best served by ratting out high-ranking Nazi officials helping to develop rocket science. As such, the Iron Tzars took a stance early on that anyone in this club had to be a lifer. There is no leaving. No divorce for any of us. Not just you. If we decide we don't want to be with you anymore, we're shit out of luck."

"That sounds miserable." Winter snapped. She turned to Roman. "If this is the way your club works, why are we pushing this so fast?" She turned back to Sting. "Explain this. What do you mean we have to be a lifer? We can't leave the club? Ever?"

"Correct. Same as our members can't leave. Even the prospects aren't cut loose. They don't cut it…"

There was a pause before Iris was the one to ask the question hanging in the air. "They don't cut it… what?"

"They die."

The woman took time to process this. Surprisingly, it was Serelda who spoke. "So, if I try to leave again, will I die?"

"You're not gonna leave again because you're with me, baby." I was not going to have her fret over this. "That's the last thing you should be concerned about, because I will make sure you never *want* to leave again. Your leaving this time was on me. I fucked up. I retrieved you, claimed you, and I'm gonna spend the rest of my life treating you like a fucking princess."

"Great. You're all gonna be so good to us we never want to leave," Iris snapped. "What are you beating around the bush over, Sting?"

In answer, Sting pulled up his shirt sleeve and pointed to a tattoo on his shoulder. The emblem matched the one on our cuts. The top rocker had the club name. The bottom Sting's name. Below that was his designation. There had been Prospect, which was now crossed out. Then member, followed by Sergeant at Arms. All had been crossed out with a single line.

Now, President took their place. "You have to get inked. Yours will say *Property of Sting*."

"And why is this a thing?"

"Few reasons. First, it's club rules. Everyone here is inked. You can follow their progress within the club by their tattoo. Second, it serves as a reminder that you're Iron Tzars for life. Third, it lets everyone in the club know you're part of us. Warlock never inked or patched Bev, so we all knew he had reservations. We protected him, but Bev was on her own. Which is why Warlock tried to keep her close, even when he knew she was trying to glean information. It was the only way he had of protecting her without inking her."

"So, if we do this," Winter picked things up, "the club knows we're part of them. We'll have their protection."

"And they'll know who you belong to. We have men scattered out all over the world at any given time. It might be years before you meet some of them. When you do, there will be no mistakes. No one will hit on you. The club whores will stay away from you. You will, basically, mirror our ranks in terms of respect. You won't have a vote or be involved in the inner workings, but it will be understood that you likely know everything going on. If you give an order to a member, they will obey it as an extension of us."

"Wow." Iris raised her eyebrows in surprise. "That seems like an awful lot of power to give your women."

"It's not given lightly, baby. To make you our ol' ladies means we trust you implicitly. The three of you are the only ol' ladies in this club. It's rare a member takes a woman for this very reason."

"What about the club girls?" Serelda asked. "Are they inked?"

"Yes," Sting said without hesitation. "They have their own design, but it clearly gives our club and their designation as club whore. Once they get to the point where they want to retire from that kind of life, we find other jobs for them within the club, and their designation is changed. We aren't cruel to them, but they know in no uncertain terms what they're signing up for when they come here. They are given the rules in the strictest terms and know this is for life."

"Most become ol' ladies to interstate or international members, away from the compounds where they served," Roman added. "There have only been a few instances in the history of this club that didn't work. The vetting process is pretty extensive."

"And by a few, he means six. Not counting Bev." Sting sighed as he pulled Iris closer, pressing his forehead to hers. "We've got bad guys headed to our door, baby. This is a matter of safety. I don't want to lose you. Ever. For any reason."

"And if I refuse to be branded like cattle?"

"Baby…"

"I'm serious! What if I absolutely cannot do this, Sting?"

"I'll ask you to think about it. To really, really think hard about it. Explain to me why you can't, and we'll try to work through it."

"And if I still can't?" She was directly challenging the president. But she was also digging for the answer Sting didn't want to give.

"Then I'll figure something out. I won't lie and say everything will be fine, though. I'll have to face the other members, some of whom already want me gone. Brick and Roman will be in the same situation. If we lose that fight, they'll kill us all. You included. That's life here. The club stood by once when Warlock didn't fully claim his woman. They won't do it again. Especially since I'm his son, and I took you in as quickly as I did."

Iris was silent for a long moment, looking into Sting's eyes as if searching for something. Then she smiled. "OK. I wanted to hear it from your mouth. You didn't lie or sugarcoat it, but you laid it all out there and promised to try to make me happy." She kissed him. "I want you to always be completely honest with me. No matter how painful. In the end, I'll defer to you if it's something you can't live with, no matter what I want. I hope you'll extend the same courtesy to me."

Sting let out the breath he'd been holding. "Well. That was…"

"Anticlimactic?" Roman chuckled.

"Yeah?" Winter put her hand on his chest and shoved away from him a little. "She agreed to this. We haven't." She hiked her thumb at Serelda.

"Baby…"

"Look, I'll do it." Winter softened her tone. "But Serelda --"

"He already told me, and I'm fine with it." My woman. My little warrior. Her voice was soft but strong. "I'm Brick's. The more things I have to prove that fact the better."

I hugged her tightly, then lifted my chin and addressed my brothers. "That's my woman."

"It's not like you're in this on your own, baby," Roman added. "Brick said he was gettin' Serelda's name tattooed on the ring finger of his left hand. Like a wedding band. Me and Sting thought we'd do the same with you and Iris."

"Don't think that's getting you out of wearing a wedding band. You're only allowed to take it off for safety purposes when you're working."

"Wouldn't have it any other way." Roman grinned.

"OK. It's settled." Sting helped Iris off his lap and slapped her ass. She yelped.

"What was that for?"

"For givin' me such a hard time. Which gave me a hard-on. Now you gotta take care of it before Ace gets here to do the ink."

Iris tried to scowl at Sting but ruined it with the smile tugging at her lips. "You think so?"

"Oh, yeah. Got a use for that smart mouth of yours."

I stood, keeping Serelda in my arms as I took us to my room. I was still in the main compound but would soon move us out. There were several houses nearing completion within the fenced property grounds. The entire place was topped with razor wire, and there were guards walking the perimeter. But until we took care of this Cannibal, I was keeping Serelda inside the main clubhouse where most of the guys lived. Once she was inked, there would be a vicious wall standing between her and any danger.

Once inside my room, Serelda squirmed to get down. I thought she was about to lay into me. Berate me for the barbaric ritual I was about to subject her to. Instead, she started pulling off her clothes, eyeing me with greedy, hungry eyes.

"What are you standing there for? I need you, Brick." She lifted her chin, so like the warrior I'd named her. "Strip."

Well. When she put it that way.

Chapter Six
Serelda

What I could tell Brick hadn't realized was that I could give a good Goddamn what his club demanded I do to be his. I'd do it. If it meant getting my property patch in the form of a tattoo, fine. I'd *brand* his name on my skin if it meant I got to keep him! He'd calmed the only fears I'd really had by getting my name inked on him as well. I'd make him spell this out, though. I wanted no misunderstandings. Just not right this second. We had unfinished business we were taking care of now.

I finished stripping before Brick and reached to unfasten his pants. Muscles played beneath my fingers, and I couldn't resist bending down to kiss his muscled abdomen.

"Christ, woman!"

"Mmmm…" I sank to my knees as he shoved his jeans from his lean hips. Gripping the muscles of his ass, I took his cock deep into my mouth. I'd never thought I'd enjoy this as much as I did, but the night before had enlightened me to the power it gave me. Not only did I enjoy his taste, but the sounds he made when I sucked him sent thrills through me I never knew I craved.

"Fuck!" His hands bunched in my hair. I knew he tempered his reaction so he didn't hurt or scare me, but what he failed to realize was that there was nothing he could do that would scare me. In the short time I'd known him, Brick had literally been my rock. The man who was so gentle with me, held me when I cried, showed me the joys of sex instead of only pain and humiliation. After more than a decade of avoiding men, I'd found one man I trusted with everything I was. Brick. Xander Scott. He was my man. I was his woman. He was the vice president of Iron Tzars and needed an ol' lady to reflect his position. I wasn't there yet, but I would be. I'd be a woman he was proud to call his.

I pumped his cock while I sucked, alternately sucking the head while I stroked him, then taking him as deep as I could. He'd let me explore my limits the night before, and I found there was nothing I was opposed to with this act. Now, before he inked me, I was going to do everything I could possibly do with him before the night was over. If I was sore tomorrow, so be it. I'd deal.

"Get up, baby. Or this is gonna be over before we get started."

I looked up and met his gaze. My eyes wide-open as I took him deep once again. Very slowly, I withdrew until my mouth was around the head before sinking back down, never breaking eye contact.

"Fuck! Goddammit, Serelda! Pull back or I'm gonna put my cum down your greedy throat!"

I spread my knees where I knelt on the floor and dipped my fingers inside my pussy. I knew I was wet. Had been since the last time he'd made me orgasm that morning. When I withdrew my fingers, I offered them to Brick. He snagged my hand and took my fingers into his mouth and sucked, a defeated groan coming from his chest. Seconds later, his cock hardened even more, then he exploded.

His thighs quaked as he emptied himself down my throat. I swallowed as fast as I could, but cum leaked from the corner of my mouth. There had been a time in my life when this act terrified me beyond measure. With Brick, the second I'd had the opportunity to take him in my mouth, I'd jumped all over it.

When I'd sucked him dry, Brick sat down abruptly, his body coated in sweat, his breathing ragged.

"Fuck me," he muttered. "Never had a blowjob like that."

"I've never wanted to give one," I said softly, crawling to him and cuddling into his big, strong body. "Until you."

He squeezed me tight, turning my face up to his to kiss me. I opened my mouth to receive his tongue, letting him taste to his heart's content. The longer he kissed me, the more eager for him I got. This absolutely was not ending without him fucking me. I didn't care what happened later, but I was getting what I wanted now.

"You are perfect, Serelda. Everything about you." He spoke between deep kisses. His hands were alternately rough and gentle where he held my face and my body. It was as if he were trying to temper himself. Like he was on the verge of losing his control and was determined not to. While I knew I needed careful and gentle this first time with him, there was a sadistic part of me that wanted to see how far I could push him. Just once. To see what happened.

"I'm going to say this, Brick. You don't have to do or say anything, but I want this out now." I took a breath, knowing it was way too soon but unable to deny my feelings for this man. I didn't want to deny them. "I love you. It's not only that you make me feel safe and that you take time to calm my fears. It's *you*. Your loyalty. Your strength. Your devotion to everything you hold dear. I feel like I'm part of that inner circle, and I'm grateful. And humbled. I know you don't let many people in. Even your brothers here.

You are devoted to them and the club, but Sting is the one you follow over all others. You've made me feel like I'm part of that too. And I want you to know how much I appreciate it."

"Baby." He stroked my face tenderly before bringing his forehead to mine. "You are... everything to me. Yeah, I'll follow Sting to the ends of the earth and damn the rest to hell, but you are the one who matters most. I'll only follow Sting if I can still make sure you're protected. That changes, then mine and Sting's relationship changes. You and me are always gonna be together." He pulled back. "And just so you know? I love you too, baby."

When an embarrassing, glad cry, I wrapped my arms around his neck and hugged him as tightly as I could. His big arms wrapped around me, enclosing me in a warm blanket of protection. From the second he'd handed me those stupid Beaver Nuggets at Buc-ee's when me and Winter had stowed away in Roman's truck, I'd known Brick was the man for me.

He urged me to straddle him, then he stood. The raw power in his body never ceased to amaze me. "Now. You wanted me to fuck you? That's what you're gonna get, little warrior." He carried me to the bed, planted a knee, then laid me down gently, never separating from me. "This first time, I'm gonna be as gentle as I can be. If you feel the first little twinge of pain, you stop me. Understand? I absolutely will not hurt you, Serelda. I mean it."

"You're not going to." I ran my hands down his flanks to grip his ass. His muscles played under my palms as I touched him. Which was something else I'd never get enough of. His responses to my touch. His hard body moving underneath my hands. "I can't wait to feel you inside me!" I was anxious to get to it. My body shook with the adrenaline rush I was getting.

"Ain't using a rubber, Serelda. Nothing comes between us."

I cocked my head. "Why would you want to?"

That got a bark of laughter from him. "Well, I've been in prison for one thing. But I'm clean. I didn't fuck or get fucked in prison and I've never taken a woman bareback, and I get tested once a year because of the prison ink. Nothing has ever come back bad. I wouldn't even consider this if it had."

"I haven't been with a man since..."

He kissed me. Hard. Sweeping his tongue inside my mouth, Brick kissed me until my senses were scrambled and I was moaning and writhing beneath him.

"You ready for me, little warrior?"

"More than you'll ever know, Brick. Make me yours!"

"Oh, baby. You already are. This just gives me a chance to put my baby in there so you can't ever fuckin' leave me again."

Watching my face carefully, Brick slid inside me in one smooth glide. I gasped for breath, my mouth open, my eyes wide and firmly fixed on Brick's. Then he slid out. When he thrust forward again, I cried out. That wonderful pleasure I always found in his arms hovering on the edge of my sanity. And this promised to eclipse anything else I'd ever felt.

"Brick!" I clutched his ass, digging my nails into the muscled globes. "Oh, God! Brick!"

When he thrust inside me for the third time, I came. Fragmented into a billion pieces. I screamed, arching my back off the bed, holding my pelvis against him as hard as I could to take him as deeply as possible.

"Fuck! Serelda! Fuckin' squeezing my cock like a fuckin' vise! AHH!" Sweat coated us both. While I let go and embraced my orgasm, Brick was valiantly trying to fight his off. "I will not come. I will not come..." He chanted his mantra over and over, shaking his head, sending beads of sweat flying over me.

I rocked back and forth, my thighs moving over him where they draped over his bent legs. "More!" Brick sat back on his heels, gripping my hips to hold me still, but I wasn't going to be denied. "I said more!"

"Baby, hold still. I can't... I'm gonna come if you keep this up!"

"Fuck me, Brick!" I could feel another building orgasm. The pleasure was nearly too much, but after a lifetime of pain, I was greedy for the pleasure. "Do it! Do it now!"

"I said still!" He swatted my outer thigh with one huge hand. The bite of pain was like throwing gasoline on a fire. I came in a violent, wet rush, screaming his name. I thrust my hips at him, grinding on his cock as I took what he refused to give me as fast as I wanted it. "Fuck!"

With a roar and another smack to my thigh, Brick jerked himself out of me, gripping my hips and flipping me to my belly. Before I could get my knees under me, he blanketed me with his heavier frame, his cock poking at my pussy before surging home.

"I told you to fuckin' hold still, woman!" His growl in my ear sounded out of control and as hungry as I was. "You will do what I fuckin' tell you to!"

"Give me what I want, and I'll consider it." I have no idea where this bravado was coming from. This wasn't me. But, by God, it was freeing! I'd never felt so alive in my life! I wiggled my ass underneath him, reminding him he was buried good and deep inside me and I was ready for the fucking he'd promised me.

"I'm so fucked." He mashed me to the bed and drove his cock inside me with ever-increasing strength and speed. I leaned my head against one arm where he'd braced himself on the bed. I rubbed my face against him, kissing his biceps in praise. He grunted and continued the brutal pace I'd demanded of him.

It wasn't long before he swelled inside me. The new position didn't allow for friction on my clit and kept me from coming and taking him with me. Brick must have known that, because the second I felt his dick growing larger, he wrapped one arm around me to find my clit.

"Now, you little witch," he growled in my ear. "Now you'll fuckin' come for me. I'm comin' with you, and you're gonna take my cum in this sweet pussy."

"Brick!" I screamed my orgasm, his words and clever fingers taking me over the edge into madness. Nothing had ever felt this good. It was raw. Brutal, even. But it was exactly what I wanted. What I needed.

For so long, I thought I'd never be able to handle passionate sex. Or sex at all, for that matter. I'd been so very wrong. This act, though violent in some ways, was the proof I needed that sex with someone of my choosing was so far from what I'd experienced in my past as to not even be the same act. I'd forced this situation on Brick or he'd never have done this. Even now, I knew I'd have to reassure him. Which was kind of funny when I thought about it. He'd always been the one there for me. Now I was going to be there for him.

"Fuck." He rolled us over, pulling out of me immediately. I felt the loss but was too relaxed and sated to mind too much. "Baby, come here." He didn't wait for me to roll over -- he pulled me to him, wrapping me up in his arms once again so my head rested on his shoulder. "Please tell me I didn't hurt you. God, baby! Please."

Much as I wanted to curl against him and sleep until he said it was time to get our tattoos, I gave him what I knew he needed. I raised up to brace myself on one elbow as I caressed his face with my other hand. "No, Brick. You didn't hurt me. You gave me something I desperately needed. I've never felt so much pleasure or so... alive! As I did just now." I knew I probably wasn't making any sense, but I plowed on. "I felt like a veil had been pulled from my eyes. Like the world had been in black-and-white and suddenly, I'm in Oz with all these brilliant colors and textures to explore. You gave me that, Brick. You. There was no pain. Only incredible, indescribable pleasure." Then I grinned at him. "And I expect this to be repeated. Often."

Brick let out a laugh, relief filling his face. He pulled me to him and continued to chuckle. "My beautiful, greedy little warrior. You're gonna be a handful."

"I'm going to be the vice president's ol' lady. Sting laid it out there, and I'm accepting the challenge. You need a strong woman at your side. That's me."

"It certainly is, baby."

"Now. If you're done with thinking I'm all fragile and shit, I want to curl up around your hard, muscled body and take a nap before I wear your ink. Then afterward, I want to get drunk and have more wicked sex. I've got a lot to make up for, and I expect to get what I want."

"Fuck... I'm so fuckin' fucked." He groaned, but

I saw the smile on his lips.

* * *

Brick

Instead of being the shrinking violet everyone expected her to be, I thought Serelda and Iris were going to fight over who got to go first. I was betting on Serelda in that fight. She was taller and with a little more bulk than Iris, though the other woman was scrappy as hell. "Want a beer? I'll grab some chairs and a bucket of peanuts if you want."

"You are two seconds away from getting Tased again, Brick." Serelda didn't even look at me when she made the threat.

"Just trying to make my president comfortable, baby."

"Drag in a pool of Jell-O, too, while you're at it." Roman grinned unrepentantly. Yeah. We were playing with fire. It was definitely worth it.

"She Tased you?" Sting tilted his head as if trying to figure out if he'd heard me right.

"She did. Then kicked me in the balls on her way out the door."

"I did not!" Serelda turned to me, outrage on her lovely face. "I kicked you in the gut!"

I shrugged. "Figured you were goin' for my balls and missed."

Her expression hardened. "Make no mistake, buddy. I hit what I aim for. If I'd been goin' for your balls, they'd still be singing."

Sting and Roman burst out laughing. Poor Ace wasn't sure what to think.

"If this is what all ol' ladies are going to be like, I say we take a vote to ban them all," Ace said with his gloved hands raised in surrender. "Anyone who thought bikers were vicious never met their women."

That got Iris and Serelda to giggling and they embraced warmly. "I'm going to love you, Iris," Serelda said as they parted. "As the president's woman, I'll defer to you. You can get the needle in your arm first." That last was a parting shot, and we all knew it. Especially when Iris swallowed visibly.

"Yeah. Thanks." She shook her head and took the seat Ace had prepared. "What the fuck was I thinking?"

Serelda sat beside her and took her hand. "You can do this. Just a brief bit of pain, and it's done. You're the president's woman, Iris." She grinned. "You got this."

Iris nodded once, then shifted her gaze to Sting and put her chin up. "Yeah. I got this."

It took about an hour and a half for each woman's tattoo. Ace helped Iris pick out a design first, then set to work. When he was done, there was a purple iris flower with yellow ends on the petals on Iris's inner wrist with the words "Property of" arched over the top and "Sting" in elegant scripted large letters beneath it. Iris smiled down at the new ink on her arm with a soft expression.

"It's beautiful, Ace. Thank you."

"My pleasure. Want your name on your man's finger in the same script?"

She glanced up at Sting. "I suppose that's his choice."

"No, baby. I'm givin' you that decision. This is all for you and the other women. We're followin' the rules of the club but makin' sure it's all about you and your sisters here. You choose the tattoos we get."

"Awww," Winter sighed. "That's so sweet!"

"I think I'm gonna barf," Ace deadpanned. "And

don't think I ain't tellin' the guys. This is too good not to."

"Tell 'em anything you want, you bastard." Roman chuckled. "My girl's worth it."

I grunted. Serelda was making me proud as fuck. God, I loved that woman!

She was next, choosing an intricate knotted bracelet for her tattoo. Her inner wrist was where Ace placed the text. Serelda chose a bold, masculine font for my name, so at odds with the delicate bracelet she'd picked for herself. Ace did my ring in a similar style but had done her name on the outside of my finger along the length.

I wanted to go, to take my woman back and show how proud I was to be her man, but knew she'd want to stay while her sister was inked. Winter chose a butterfly in pale blue with monarch markings resting on pale blue roses on her inner wrist. Ace had woven Roman's name within the markings on the butterfly while the property declaration sat proudly above the butterfly. Roman's ring had Winter's name in a delicate script with tiny thorns drawn into the lettering at random places.

"Well," Ace said as he stretched, taking off his sixth pair of gloves with a snap. "When Wylde told me what I had waitin' on me when I got home, I dreaded this whole thing. I can honestly say I've never enjoyed a job more. You ladies will definitely be a welcome addition to Iron Tzars. I'll spread the word."

Serelda wrapped her arms around my neck before nuzzling my chest. I clutched her to me, my chin up in pride. "You're my woman, Serelda. Got the ink to prove it."

"I'm glad I finally convinced you." She giggled.

"Honey, you didn't need to convince me. I knew

the second I saw you, you were the one for me."

"You didn't think I could handle you."

"Well, that's something you cured me of a few hours ago."

She raised her face to mine. "Want to reinforce the idea?"

Instead of answering her, I scooped her up and urged her legs around my waist as I hurried out of the room. "Text me if you need me, Sting. Got shit to do."

"Same, brother. We'll meet tomorrow unless Wylde has something before then."

I glanced over my shoulder to see Roman and Winter kissing like they had the same thing on their minds. Looked like it was going to be a good night all the way around.

Chapter Seven
Serelda

Brick and I made love all night. Literally. We might have napped for an hour or so between rounds, but every time one of us would wake, we were all over each other. I lost count of how many mind-blowing orgasms I had. Brick finally called mercy around dawn, and I patted him on the chest in sympathy.

"I know it's going to be hard on you keeping up with your young, hot wife, but honestly, I expected more for our first night together."

That got me fucked again. This time with feeling. God, I was having so much fun!

I woke late in the morning, but Brick was nowhere to be found. There was a note on my phone by the bedside letting me know he was meeting with Wylde, Sting, and Roman and to make myself at home. I knew where Winter and Iris's rooms were and figured I'd start there.

I dressed quickly, throwing my hair into a ponytail. I might have stood in front of the mirror for a hot minute admiring the vest with my property patch on the back, but I'd never admit it to Brick. He'd said I had to wear it any time I left our room, and I figured I needed to know how I looked in it. For some reason, the sight of my scars didn't bother me today. They were part of me and obviously didn't bother Brick in the least. In fact, he'd traced several of them with his tongue last night. Besides, with the biker chick vibe going on, they were kind of badass.

When I opened the door to go find my sister and Iris, both women were at my door. Winter had her hand raised to knock, and all three of us jumped before dissolving into giggles.

"I can't believe you slept so late, Serelda." Winter looped her arm through mine and Iris's as we made our way to the big party room. During the day, there was always food and a big-screen TV on. Usually with something sports-related. Today was no exception.

"Oh? How long you guys been up?" I had a feeling not long.

"Forever. We got tired of waiting on you." Iris tried to look all innocent, but I wasn't fooled.

"Well, I was busy last night. Didn't get *any* sleep."

"Really? I slept like a baby." Winter gave a superior sigh, as if she were so sad for me. I gave her the side eye.

"That's too bad, Winter. I'd have hoped your man would have taken care of you after all you went through for him." I grinned. "Mine certainly did."

Winter gasped. "Serelda! You little slut!"

I couldn't help it. I giggled like a loon. "I totally am. And you know what? I loved every fucking second of it."

We all laughed as we made our way to the bar where there were snacks and pizza for the game. Apparently, we'd missed breakfast.

"I never thought I could be this happy," I said, looking at Winter. I knew my sister would understand. "When I thought I couldn't have Brick, I wanted to make sure you had your happy ever after without having to worry about me."

She reached over and gripped my hand. "We're family, Serelda. My life will never be complete without you in it. And Iris is now part of that family, too. We have to stick together if we have even a chance of taking some of the burdens off our men."

"I know." Winter shook her head. "I worry about

Sting sometimes. He never shows it, but I know he worries he'll lead the club wrong. He never wants to be the one to hurt the club."

"He won't be," I said softly. "He's got good men supporting him. Brick's his VP, and they always talk things out if it's a major decision. Besides, I saw what happened at Black Reign. With the club member they... expelled." I kept my voice low, looking around me in case we weren't alone. There were a few members milling around, but they mostly ignored us. I still didn't want to talk too loudly. "He took his time deciding what he needed to do. He and Brick talked it over. I heard him say he didn't want to make a permanent decision while he was angry. No. Your man will do right by this club. And you."

Iris's lips parted in a small gasp. "Thank you for that. It means a lot."

"We have good men," Winter said, growing serious. "It's our job to take care of them and to ease as many of their burdens as we can. We'll need to stay in this together."

"We'll have each other's backs as well as theirs." Iris put her chin up. "We're their last line of defense."

"You know what this means, right?" I gripped my sister's hand.

"Yeah. We have to be part of whatever they're planning. We brought this evil to their door. We'll take responsibility for it."

"Pretty sure we already had that conversation." Sting's voice was soft as he came up behind us. "The answer was no."

"I'm not talking about us actually doing the fighting," I said, trying to reason with the man. "But we need to know what's going on so we know how best to help you."

"Tinkerbell, I appreciate what you're saying." Brick wrapped an arm around my shoulders and kissed my temple. "But the best thing the three of you can do -- especially you and Winter -- is stay where we tell you to stay. The club can take this guy and whoever he throws at us, but if we're distracted worrying about where you are and if you're in the line of fire, we're liable to make mistakes that could get people killed."

"What did you find out, Sting?" Iris asked, deflected the conversation. She was young, but she was already learning the art of diplomacy.

"There are five men on their way to Indiana. We had Wylde reach out and tell them we had you. He told them he'd only hand you over to the Cannibal himself. That way we get the maximum payout and not a portion. It's a plausible reason and gives this psycho incentive to come out of hiding. If he wants you bad enough, he'll show. If not, we'll figure something else out. We're counting on the two of you to identify him, because we can't."

"What about Brick?" I asked. "If they've put out a hit on you, won't they think this is a trap?"

"It *is* a trap, baby. This is what we do. They're saying they'll sacrifice me since I put the club in danger by killing outside our territory. We've got it all under control."

"By bringing them here, we can better control the situation. When they die, we can make sure the bodies are never found." Sting spoke softly, but directly to his woman. Not to me or Winter.

Winter looked fierce when she glanced at me. I knew what she was thinking but absolutely would not entertain the possibility Brick or Roman would betray us.

"Don't even think it, Winter," Roman snapped. "You know better."

"What?" Brick looked from me to Winter before a pained expression crossed his face. "You don't believe that, Tinkerbell." His voice was husky, and I could tell even the thought that I believed he could betray me hurt him deeply. He didn't often call me by that nickname. Only when he was trying to soothe me.

"No, Brick. I don't believe it. Not after what you and the men had us do to secure our safety. Winter doesn't believe it either, Roman. She's just being cautious. I promise you she's more worried about me than she is about herself."

"So, it's me she doesn't trust." Brick made it a statement as he looked from me to Winter.

Winter sighed. "I trust you, Brick. Hell, I even suggested earlier that you get them to come here. I'm sorry. It was a fleeting thought. No more."

Brick nodded. "I understand. It's my life they want. But, understand me, I'll gladly give them my life if it keeps the two of you safe."

"No," I said firmly. "You won't. And if you ever say anything like that again, I *will* kick you in the balls." I looked at the men, giving them the hardest, most unyielding look I could. "We will *all* come out of this alive and together or not at all."

"You guys said we were in this for life, and that's exactly how this is going to work." Iris stuck her chin up. "We will follow your lead. Do exactly what you say because you're the president, Sting. Brick is vice president. Roman is your enforcer. *We* are your women. So you better fucking remember that when shit goes down. Because we will stand by you no matter how rough things get."

"And we'll kill any motherfucker trying to come

after you." Winter's voice was soft but carried no less impact. These women meant business.

I stepped close to Brick but didn't reach for him. When he tried to pull me into his arms, I batted him away. "No one is expendable. We're all a team. You will kill these fuckers and send a fucking message to this Cannibal person that he's next."

A crowd had gathered loosely around us. Several of the younger members looked amused. The older ones raised eyebrows but nodded in what seemed like approval.

"Can't argue with that." Atlas nodded like he was satisfied with the conversation. "These women are gonna fit right in."

"I damn sure approve," someone said. I didn't see who.

"Same."

"Sting, this is how it's supposed to be. They know the full score?"

"They do, Blaze. They know everything expected of them and the consequences."

"Good. I was worried when Brick's woman split. Seems he worked things out with her."

"I did. They're all inked and have their vests. It's done." Brick threw one big arm around my shoulders casually. It was a show of ownership, and I knew it. Maybe it made me weird, but I kind of liked the caveman gesture.

"Guys?" Wylde stuck his head out of a room off to the side. "They say they'll be here in three days, but I've got them pegged just outside of town. Might want to assume we're gonna have company very soon."

Instantly, every single man in the room checked his sidearm, then headed out of the room. I assumed it was to their various posts. No one had to give an order.

Just the information there could be trouble headed this way was order enough.

I took a breath. This was it. One way or another, there were several sons of bitches who were going to die tonight. I only hoped the man who'd tortured me and my sister was one of them. And I hoped to fucking God I got to deliver the killing blow.

* * *

Brick

God, I had a fierce ol' lady! She gathered the other women, and they spoke at length. Finally, Iris hugged both Winter and Serelda before leaving their group. She came to Sting and wrapped her arms around his middle.

"I'm going to take the children to the basement to keep them out of the way in case things get out of hand." She slid one hand up his chest to his face, where she bunched her hand in his beard and tugged so she had his full attention. "Things will *not* get out of hand. You hear me? You get so much as a scratch, I will be supremely pissed."

Sting gave her a cocky smirk. "As you wish, Buttercup."

Iris scowled at him before tugging even harder until their lips met. It was a hard, passionate kiss. One that spoke of the fear Iris was trying to hide behind aggression.

One thing I'd noticed about the president's woman was that she was generally passive. Until it was time to be otherwise. She'd proven that when she'd sat for three months listening to us plan her sister's rescue, then took matters into her own hands when she thought we were backing off. With the addition of Winter and Serelda, Iris was learning how to be the president's ol' lady. The sisters were not only taking back their lives, but the determination they both showed to take the fight to anyone who needed it was a great model for Iris. Which was to say, Iris was a force to be reckoned with.

"Well," I said, not looking at Sting. It was hard not to smirk at the other man. "I guess you have your orders, prez."

"I do."

"God help you if you defy them." My remark got a startled laugh from Sting. One glance at Serelda, and I knew she'd heard the exchange. I winked at her. She acknowledged me with a slight nod. No doubt she was wound up and determined to do whatever needed doing. Including facing her nightmare. So was Winter. Both women sat calmly, talking quietly. Serelda never took her gaze from me. That woman was ready. And she wasn't backing down. Sweet Jesus, I was hard as a motherfucker!

"You were right, Wylde." Shooter's voice came through our earpieces. He was a Marine sniper in his former life. Now he served as our lookout when we were expecting trouble. No one was better at spotting trouble than Shooter. "Incoming. Three big-ass SUVs comin' in with no lights. Hard to say from here how many people total, but I'm sure there's more than six." It had only been six hours since Wylde had made contact with these motherfuckers.

"Three days, my ass." Atlas shook his head, muttering as he put his eye to the scope of his M4A1 rifle. "Let them come."

"How's this gonna work, Prez?" I always led any situation when it was imperative the men follow Sting's orders to the letter. Most were good, but there were still a few holdouts. With everyone in battle positions, I spoke using the throat mic on the team's secure frequency so everyone could hear. I wouldn't be able to see their faces and judge the dissents, but I could throw my weight behind Sting to let everyone know I was solidly in his corner.

"Shooter, assign targets, but everyone will hold until Brick or myself gives the word. I intend on killin' these bastards, but not before I have every scrap of information I can get. We absolutely are not leaving the Cannibal alive."

"Copy." Every member of the team acknowledged one by one.

"Scram." That was the signal for certain members to switch their radios to a different frequency, and I followed suit. It was a private channel specifically for his inner circle to use to communicate privately. Which was a sore spot with a few of our members.

"Wylde, I have a couple questions for ya." Sting's voice was calm, but there was something just that little bit off. "How long do you think these bastards were here before you contacted them?"

"Given the speed with which they moved, I'd say a while. They had to have had time to study us. Comin' here this fast would be suicide or stupidity otherwise. Given that Brick killed one of their men on a bus full of people and walked away, they had to know we were connected and dangerous. You're welcome, by the way. I got the cops off the trail and led them to a crashed motorcycle fifteen miles away from the shooting. No bodies, but I left enough crumbs for them to go straight to a group of small-time arms dealers we'd tagged to get rid of."

"Good. Next question. How'd they know where to find Brick?"

Wylde didn't miss a beat. "I assume whoever told him Brick had killed his man told him. Because even the police don't know who did that killin', and they were there within ten minutes."

"I'm sure people got cell phone images of it. If not the actual killin', then afterward. Brick said he and Serelda didn't exactly rush away from the scene." Sting was covering all the bases, and I saw where he was going with this.

"Sure. There were pics and vids posted and sent all over the place. Fortunately, I have some snazzy-ass software Giovanni was having me test out that searches the web media I designate and obliterates it. In this case, I took the time and location along with images of Serelda and Brick and plugged it into the system. Giovanni and me got a handle on it in less than half an hour. While no software of this kind is a hundred percent, we're talking about Giovanni Romano and Argent Tech. No. Images of that incident didn't get out to the Cannibal. He was *informed*." The emphasis on the word "informed" left no doubt about Wylde's opinion of what had happened or where it came from.

"Only the Iron Tzars knew who Brick was," Sting said in a soft, deadly voice.

"Yep," Wylde agreed in a cheerful voice. "Good thing I'm the motherfuckin' tech guy."

Wylde knew who did this. Who had ratted out the club.

"Atlas, is the kill box ready?"

"Absolutely, prez. Ready for several days of work. However long you want this to take."

"A long fuckin' time, Atlas."

There was silence on the radio. At first, I wondered who Sting suspected, but then I realized he was confirming what he already knew. We met and locked gazes. When I shook my head slightly, he said, "Takes a maniac to catch a maniac…"

Maniac. He was one of the oldest members of Iron Tzars and had called for Warlock's patch more than once while he was with Bev. He hadn't voiced his opposition to Sting becoming president, but he hadn't given his support either. Overall, he'd kept quiet. Keeping his head down, as it were. He'd done everything anyone had asked of him since I'd taken over without question or comment. But this didn't surprise me one bit.

"When this is over, I want everyone not on this channel rounded up and taken to the barn. Every one of you keep an eye on everyone else. I want a full and complete report of who did what and to what degree. Anyone hanging back without express orders, I want to know about it. Anyone missin' a target or killing without permission, I want to know that too. Discord in this club because of Warlock's actions and my taking over ends tonight. Even if I have to kill every single motherfucker in here."

There were eight people on the channel, including me. A very small core group of men Sting trusted with his life. I'd helped him make this list when he first realized he was going to have to do something about Warlock. Some were officers like Wylde and Atlas, while others were patched members holding the line, so to speak. They were simply there because Sting and I trusted them. Not to be a special kill squad or to rat out their brothers. This was the first time Sting had ever given such an order. To the man, they all sounded off strong and clear. Just like I knew they would.

It wasn't long before the SUVs smashed through the fence on the edge of our property. There was a dirt road leading through a large field that eventually made its way to the back of the main compound. Our group switched back to the main channel.

"Here they come," Shooter said. "They're drivin' like they're gonna shoot first and ask questions later."

"No kill shots!" Sting barked out as he snagged his own rifle. "I want every single motherfucker in those cages alive!"

The shooting started before the SUVs had fully stopped. The men inside were out and shooting at anything they saw or thought might hide a potential target. The Iron Tzars stood their ground, aiming at legs and feet when men exited the vehicles. The cages themselves had the tires shot out to prevent them from leaving. Windows shattered, and some of the intruders climbed back inside the relative safety of the trucks while others riddled the clubhouse with bullets.

Sting had flipped over the heavy oak table in the center of the room where Winter and Serelda were and crouched behind it until the women were settled. Neither sister looked scared -- rather, they both looked furious. Like they were about to kill a motherfucker.

I fired several times out of the window toward two sets of feet on the ground behind the doors of the SUV. Hit one, and the guy screamed before climbing back into the truck. When I glanced back at my girl, Serelda snagged the gun from Sting's hip as he darted from the table to the window on the other side of the main door.

"My woman snagged your sidearm," I yelled to him over the sporadic gunfire.

"Yeah. Felt it. She good?"

"Seems to be." I found Roman farther down the length of the room, his rifle on the window ledge as he fired off two rounds. Another man yelped, this one going down clutching his shoulder. "Roman! Your girl need a weapon?"

He shook his head. "Not if you want any of these fuckers alive. She'll kill anything she shoots at."

"Hmm," Sting muttered, looking back at Serelda. My woman leveled her gaze on him as if daring him to take his gun back. "Yeah. Hadn't thought of that." He raised his voice. "Serelda, don't you kill anyone."

"No promises, Sting."

Chapter Eight
Brick

"Come on," Sting said, a maniacal gleam filling his eyes. "How can I expect the men to follow my instructions if my own vice president's woman won't?"

She sighed, throwing him a frustrated look. "Fine. But I'm gonna be there when you kill these fuckers."

"Never said you couldn't be, darlin'." Sting grinned at her.

"Watch it, brother. She's my woman."

"So? Iris is mine."

"Serelda ain't your darlin'." I knew what my brother meant, but the tension needed breaking before we killed these fuckers too fast. Breaking the tension in a firefight was damned hard to do.

Sting laughed. "Man, those three women are going to be the darlin's of everyone here. They are fuckin' fierce. And they will rule this place if we let them."

I rubbed the back of my neck and muttered, "Kinda thought they already did."

"Total of twelve men, Sting," Shooter confirmed. "All twelve are either under the vehicles or in them."

"Good." Sting put a fresh clip in his rifle before raising his voice to address our visitors. "Toss your fuckin' weapons away from the vehicles." Silence. No one complied, but no one spoke either.

"Probably talkin' amongst themselves. Tryin' to form a plan." Roman kept his eyes firmly on the enemy as he spoke. "We can't safely approach them until they comply. I mean, we could, but that would mean some of 'em'd die."

"No one dies," Sting reiterated. "Not yet."

Wylde broke the silence through our earwigs. "They're hurt, Sting. No one's dead, but there are a couple hurt bad enough they'll need medical attention soon."

"You hacked into their vehicle?"

I could almost see Wylde's superior smirk. "Of course. Their phones too."

"Smug bastard." Roman chuckled, shaking his head.

"One of 'em's on the phone to their boss." Wylde sobered immediately, his voice now quiet and even. "He wants them to storm us, but they're tellin' him they're too shot up. He's callin' 'em all kinds of stupid while they're callin' him a son of a bitch. Blah blah blah. I don't think they're in any shape to make a final stand outside of suicide, and these guys are hired muscle. They ain't dyin' for this bastard."

"He close?" Sting held my gaze while Roman eased his way in our direction, careful of the windows.

"Just outside the compound. Not sure if he intended to come in after these guys had finished with this or if they were bringing the women to him, but the person they're communicating with is outside the fence a hundred yards from where these fuckers broke through."

"He alone?"

"Yep. Watchin' the shootout. If we're gonnna get the bastard, might want to before he gets the hell outta Dodge."

"Morgue. Smoke. Go collect the bastard and meet us in the barn."

"On it, prez." The two big men disappeared out the door and off in the direction Wylde instructed. Sting waited a few minutes before giving the team the go ahead. Then we advanced on the vehicles. We jerked open the doors, disarming anyone we found. More than one of them had gotten shot in the legs during the exchange. Not only did we want them alive, but it had been the only target to aim at with them behind the car door while they engaged us. Couple of them would be lucky to make it to the barn before they bled out. That was on me, because I didn't hold the men back.

We tied tourniquets above the wounds on a couple of the men, but we weren't overly careful with them. They were going to die. Just not until Sting said so.

Fifteen minutes later, we convened in a big barn. It was deceptive in that it looked old and rundown on the outside, but the structure was sturdy and had a smooth concrete floor. A thick tarp was spread around the area where our prisoners hung suspended by their wrists from chains draped over rafters above their heads.

"This shouldn't take too long, but I'm kinda hopin' it does." Sting stood in front of our guests, off the tarp with his arms crossed over his chest. He gave the men an amused grin. "Boys, you in a heap a trouble."

"Look. We were paid to do a job. Surely you can understand that." One of the men was trying to be reasonable, but he was sweating, the pulse beating furiously at his neck. He knew what was happening and trying to deny it to himself.

"You came into our home, guns blazing." Sting chuckled. "What did you expect was gonna happen?"

"We were told you were giving up the man who killed one of our guys. That and you were sending the girl back."

"He told us to ask if you had the other one, too.

He knows they both came here, and he wants them back." The guy was obviously trying to ignore the whole situation. Like he thought we'd all become friends and do what his boss wanted without question.

Sting looked back at me. "Are they for real?"

I shrugged. "Dunno. Son?" I addressed the second guy. "You *do* realize you're not leavin' here alive. Right?"

"What?" Poor guy's eyes went wide and round in alarm. He truly was a dumbass.

One of the others grunted. "I'll take what I'm owed, but please, for the love of God, don't make me die next to this fuckin' dumbass."

"I can understand your frustration, but the rules are --"

"Yeah, yeah. Ride with a dumbass, die with a dumbass." He sighed. "Just tell me what you need to know so we can get this over with."

"Wow." Roman scrubbed a hand over his neck. "Wasn't expecting common sense."

"My loyalty is to money. Where I'm goin', I ain't gonna need it. I ain't going to be tortured if I can avoid it. That means I spill my guts, that's what I'm doin'."

The first guy pissed himself and whimpered, but thankfully didn't beg. I'd have hated to gag a man for begging for his life, but I'd do it. The mere fact he'd been in this group, no matter what his involvement, negated his getting to live.

About that time, Smoke shoved a man inside the room. His hands were zip-tied behind his back, and there was a hood over his head. Must have been gagged too because his voice was muffled, and he wasn't able to form intelligible words. Morgue followed soon after, shutting and locking the door behind him.

"That one's a real freak," Morgue said, pointing at their captive. "He was nibbling on this." Morgue tossed what looked like a strip of fried pork skin inside a plastic bag to Sting. "I'm not an expert, but I'm pretty sure that's not pig skin."

For a moment, what Morgue was saying didn't register. "Who gives a fuck what it is?" I shook my head. "Why would I care what this pissant had for a snack?"

Morgue leveled a look on me, his expression flat when I was sure he was more than a little frustrated with my answer. "Brick. Think about it. His name's the Cannibal."

I glanced at Sting, then Roman. Roman went white, then his face flushed red and his gaze turned murderous. He approached the guy and whipped off the hood. Morgue and Smoke tossed a chain over the rafters and fastened his wrist to it with thick cuffs. They pulled the chain until his feet dangled a couple of inches above the floor like the others. Roman waited patiently for his answer when I knew he wanted to kill the motherfucker.

"Whatcha snackin' on?" Roman's grin wasn't pleasant. His tone made it sound like he was really interested when it was obvious he was on the edge of killing.

"Number One." His eyes were wild, and his gaze darted continuously around the room. He looked like he might be high. "I've already consumed all I had of Number Two."

Roman tilted his head to the side, trying to work out what the crazy bastard meant. "The fuck?"

"He means me, Roman." *Winter.* I'd forgotten the women were anywhere close. I hadn't accompanied Serelda or her sister, but I'd known they were going to be here. They'd insisted. Normally, that wouldn't have swayed Sting if he thought it wasn't in their best interest, but he needed the women to confirm this Cannibal was the one who'd terrorized them thirteen years ago.

"What?" Roman turned to his wife, stepping away from the guy automatically. When torturing someone, it's best to not get too close when you're distracted. These people knew they were going to die, so they had nothing to lose.

"Me. I'm Number One." Winter held out her wrist for Roman to see. I moved to look, and my blood froze.

"I thought that was the letter 'I.'" Roman shook his head, obviously not believing what he was seeing.

Then Serelda stepped forward as well, her other arm held out for me. Her gaze was fastened on the Cannibal. "I'm Number Two." On her wrist, a scar I'd traced with my lips many times since we'd become intimate, was the Roman numeral two.

I looked up at Serelda, horror washing through me like a tidal wave. My grip on her wrist tightened, and I pulled her to me. Roman went so far as to pick up Winter and head toward the door with her.

"Roman, put me down." Winter's voice was soft, but insistent.

"No fuckin' way, Winter. Out you go."

"Roman." Something in Winter's voice must have clued Roman in to the fact that his woman wasn't leaving. He stopped and gave her a frustrated look, his jaw ticking like a son of a bitch.

"No, Winter. I'm not givin' you this."

"Yes, you are. You're going to put me down and let me be with my sister."

I wanted to tell Winter that she and her sister

could be together. Outside the barn. But I knew better. Neither woman would leave until they were good and ready.

Serelda opened her mouth, probably to agree with her sister, but I leaned in to kiss her. "I know, little warrior. Sting let you in. He'll have to be the one to put you out."

"Way to throw a brother under the bus, asshole," Sting groused but didn't look angry. Just frustrated.

"My woman wants vengeance, she's gettin' it," I said. "One thing I've learned is that Serelda is stronger than she thought she was."

"Don't you mean, than *you* thought she was?" Roman had Winter wrapped tightly in his arms, obviously not liking her being here with something as monstrous as a man who'd been calmly eating fried pieces of her skin.

"No. I knew from the moment I met her she was a fierce warrior. She was letting her wounds heal before she went for revenge."

Serelda looked up at me like I'd hung the moon. The very last place in the world I wanted my woman to be was here in this moment with these bastards. My club was here to protect her, but no one could protect her from nightmares. The only thing restraining me from shutting her securely outside this barn was knowing she needed this. She was strong enough to either do what she needed to, or to watch us do it for her.

"You're a wonderful man, Xander. Thank you for letting me do this even though I know you don't want me to."

"You're the VP's ol' lady, Serelda. Anyone underestimates you at their own peril. Honey, that ain't me." I met and held her gaze. Serelda's chin went up and her shoulders back. In that moment, she was every bit the equal of any man in that barn.

Serelda turned and addressed Sting. "I have no idea if this guy is crazy or if he's trying to fuck with us, but this is one of the men who tortured us thirteen years ago. He's the one who was more methodical." She held her wrist out to Sting for him to see. Winter did the same.

"Serelda always tried to take his attention away from me." Winter's voice was soft as she spoke, her gaze on the Cannibal never wavering. She looked like prey, keeping an eye on the predator, trying to decide if she needed to get to safety.

"He fixated on Winter," Serelda explained. "I knew if I didn't do something, he'd do more than just scar her."

The women stood shoulder to shoulder, clasping hands as they faced the man who'd haunted them for more than a decade. Serelda got close to him, tilting her head to the side as if trying to size him up. The guy had a look of wonder on his face, like he was face-to-face with his greatest dream.

"Number Two? My lovely, delicioussssss girl." He looked and sounded like he was euphoric. Clearly, he wasn't right. "I'll pick you over my Number One this time. Just…" He licked his lips. "Just one little taste…"

One of the guys hanging from the rafters puked. Violently. I knew the feeling.

"We're gonna fuckin' die."

I thought that was the guy who'd tried to reason with us earlier. Sounded like he understood now.

"Yeah." That was the guy who'd offered to cooperate for a quick death. "Maybe we should. This guy's a sicko."

"I don't want to die..." The man broke down, sobbing softly. He didn't beg, though. Guess he was smarter than I first thought. Just not smart enough to not accept money for kidnapping someone.

"Life is a series of choices," Serelda said, turning her gaze to the wimpy guy. "Sometimes, you choose death whether you realize it at the time or not."

"Honey, anyone choosing to prey on women or children is begging for death." Sting gripped Serelda's shoulder. "When they do, it's up to men like us to give them what they're askin' for."

Serelda nodded slowly. "Yes. I, for one, am grateful."

Sting dropped his hand, looking at the men we'd lined up. He pointed to the practical one. "Save him for later. I have some questions for him before he dies. As I remember it, Winter and Serelda specified there were two men who tortured them."

The man nodded. "I've worked for this guy for a long time. I'm not sure if the man I remember is the one you're talking about, but if you'll promise me a quick death, I'll tell you what I know."

"Already said a quick death was your reward. Just thought you'd like this time to prepare."

He shrugged. "Waiting is sometimes its own torture."

Sting pursed his lips, obviously trying to make up his mind. Then he nodded once. "Deal. Tell me."

"His name was Sigmund Mural. He had a thing about blood." The guy glanced at Serelda before dropping his gaze.

"Sig..." Serelda whispered. "That's what he called the man." Serelda nodded to the Cannibal. "He cut us in patterns, deeper than just the top layer of skin. Sig preferred shallow cuts. Just enough to make us bleed."

Serelda had gone pale, and Winter looked like she either wanted to kill someone or throw up. Instead of doing either, she threw her shoulders back much like Serelda had and schooled her features. Our women were determined to see this through to the end.

The guy winced, knowing the trauma he was causing. He met my gaze, and I nodded.

"Finish it," I said. "Your end will be up to Sting."

He nodded. "He would... he would cut the women he was given in shallow cuts, like she said. When he did, he'd..." He cleared his throat. "He'd play with them. Said he liked the feel of blood making his body and that of the women slide together. The more blood, the better. When the women got close to dying, he'd cut a major artery and cover himself in the blood as he held the girl until she bled out."

"Where is he?" This was Sting's room, but I couldn't help making the demand.

"Dead." The guy nodded toward the Cannibal. "He..."

"Oh, God." Winter was visibly trembling now. I thought it was telling that the usually unflappable Winter had deferred to her sister. This guy spooked Winter something fierce. Serelda, however, hid her emotions.

When I'd first met these women, they were meek and submissive. Since finding the men they wanted, both women had opened up and shown their true character. Serelda was as hardened as I was. Though I'd been through my trials in prison, Serelda had gone through them in her mind in the form of a demon from her past. Faced with the real flesh-and-blood man, Serelda was faring far better than I'd expected. She looked like a woman taking back her life.

"Serelda," Winter gasped, her grip on Serelda's hand tightening. She tried to tug Serelda, but my woman pulled her sister into her arms and gave her a fierce hug.

"I've got this, sister. I promised you then I'd do my best to get us out. Now, I'm promising I'll take care of this bastard like you took care of our dad."

"I don't think... Serelda, I can't..."

"Roman." Serelda found my brother's gaze. "I know you need to be here as Sergeant at Arms --"

"I've got her, Serelda. I'll take care of her."

"She doesn't like the sight of blood. It started with Sig. Ended when she killed our father."

"You can count on me. Come see her tomorrow, Serelda. Bring Brick, and we'll all do something to celebrate your freedom." Roman didn't hesitate, and Sting didn't stop him. With the most trusted inner circle here to take care of the mess, Sting was good letting Roman go.

"Take Cyrus with you, Roman. Until we take care of the other business, we always go in pairs."

"Appreciate it, prez." Roman scooped Winter up into his arms, and he and Cyrus left, closing the barn door as they left.

"Now." Sting pulled out his sidearm. "Serelda, is there anything more you need from this guy?"

"No."

With no further questions, Sting calmly shot the guy in the head. The man next to him whimpered, closing his eyes as blood sprayed over his face. More than one of the remaining men shuddered. A couple looked defiant but didn't speak. The Cannibal cackled.

Serelda stood there with a little smile on her face, her gaze fixed firmly on the crazy man. "You're gonna burn in hell, you son of a bitch."

He laughed. "Hell's too good for me, little girl. You know that."

"I do. Much as I'd love to torture you, or have these men do it, you're not worth that piece of my soul." She turned to Sting. "Thank you for letting me be here. I needed the closure."

"You're a fine ol' lady, Serelda. I'm glad you and your sister found my brothers."

"I'm glad we did too. I'm also glad to know your woman. Iris is a wonderful friend and mother. She loves those girls you adopted. She'll be a great role model for them."

"As will you and Winter. I hope my girls are as strong as the ol' ladies in this club."

"They will be." Serelda turned away from Sting and stepped into my arms. "I know you need to see this through, and then you have other matters to deal with afterward. If you'd maybe take me to our room, I can wait for you there."

"Can you give me five minutes, baby? I can have Blaze stay with you until I'm done. You can stand outside. Get some fresh air. Then I'll go and stay with you."

She shook her head. "If you want me to wait, I'll stay with you. Do what you need to do."

Yeah. She needed to be out of here. "Sting?"

"You know what's going to happen next. I know of one rat, but I suspect another."

"Lynch." I didn't hesitate. "I've suspected for a while. I can't say definitely, but my gut says he's working with Maniac."

"I had the same feeling." Atlas pulled his gun and shot two of the remaining guys. There were nine left. Then we had our own brothers to deal with. That wouldn't go as quickly.

"Well, your feelings would be right." Wylde had his laptop with him. He stepped close to Sting and showed him a screen. "Hard to believe members of this club wouldn't be smart enough to hide money better than this."

"They have it out there in the open?" Sting glanced at the computer screen, but didn't give it much more. He had no idea what he was looking at any more than I did.

"Na. Made four exchanges in three countries. It'd be decently hidden for the normal tech guy, but I'm *the* motherfucking tech guy. They didn't get past me."

"Just the two of them?"

"I checked everyone in the club. Including every person in this room, men and women alike. No one had anything to hide. They had the right amount of money. In various accounts."

"Found our secret stashes, did you?" Sting chuckled, though I knew he was anything but amused.

"They weren't secret, but I found them. I know exactly how much money everyone is supposed to have, where you put it, and how you got it. Only two who had more than they were supposed to were Maniac and Lynch. And they had *way* more than they were supposed to."

"You need more evidence?" Sting raised an eyebrow at me.

I shook my head. "If Wylde is certain, that's good enough for me."

"The rest of us can deal with this. Take Eagle with you and go see to your woman. We'll question those two fuckers to make sure, but I don't think Wylde would be wrong about more than one person. I'd be hard-pressed to say he was wrong about anything this important."

"I'm not." Wylde's usually cocky, fun-loving expression turned instantly hard. "I tried to be. But I'm not."

That was enough for me. "Send a prospect if you need me. I'll defer to you completely on this, Sting. Whatever you decide I'll support."

"You know I don't have a choice."

"They were going to sell your women back to that sadistic bastard, Sting." Wylde spoke slowly, making his point very clear as he nodded to the Cannibal. "Maniac made a deal to turn Brick over to them if they'd kill you, Sting. Text messages between him and Lynch -- on the burner phones they didn't know I knew about -- outlined their plan to get rid of you and take over the club, Maniac as president, Lynch as VP. They thought they could bring Atlas in line because of his need for money to see his mother's medical expenses met." Atlas growled, his fists bunching. "Yeah, Atlas. I knew. Also been funneling money into your mother's account at the hospital and her doctor. Sting's fully aware. The club takes care of its own. Even when our members prefer not to share."

"And this is why you're the motherfucking tech guy, Wylde." Sting shook his head. "That was supposed to be between me and you."

"I was making a point. Atlas kept this from the club, but those two followed him. They were willing to prey on our own members to get what they wanted. They don't deserve pity. Warlock wasn't a bad person. Just a man in love with the wrong woman. Maniac and Lynch are different. They betrayed their brothers for greed and power."

"Anyone have an objection?" No one spoke. "It's done, then. Atlas." Sting addressed our sergeant at arms. "Take Maniac and Lynch to the kill box. This isn't going to happen quickly."

"And the rest of these?" Atlas indicated the nine remaining men.

Sting gave them a dismissive glance. "Bring the Cannibal to the kill box. The others can die now." A couple of the prisoners whimpered or grunted, knowing it was time. One of them sobbed openly.

I turned to go. "I'll be available if you need me, but for now I'll be with Serelda."

"I'll need you in a day or two, but not now." Sting clapped me on the shoulder. "Go, brother. Eagle, escort Brick and Serelda to their room, then post up outside mine and Iris's room. Tell her I'll be there in a few hours. She can text the burner phone if she needs me."

Eagle nodded once, then we left the barn and went back to the clubhouse. It was going to be a long night. I had a lot of work to do to take Serelda's mind from the carnage taking place, and more importantly, the sick, sadistic bastard who'd literally fed off her. Fortunately, I was up to the task.

Chapter Nine
Serelda

The second we made it to our room, I bolted for the bathroom. Skidding to my knees on the tile, I vomited violently. Repeatedly. When my stomach was empty, I dry heaved for a few minutes. If I lived to be a hundred, I'd never be able to get this out of my head. That bastard had violated Winter and me in unspeakable ways. Finally, I threw my head back and screamed in rage and frustration.

"Mother fuck! Brick, I want the kill on that guy. I want to cut off his dick and make him eat *that*!"

"I know, baby. Sting will probably do exactly that. But you aren't going anywhere near that place. You've done all I'm allowing, because that bastard is too sick to taint you with even more memories. He's not fucking worth it."

"I want tattoos," I blurted out. We sat on the floor of the bathroom, and Brick held me on his lap while I finished raging. "All over my body. His marks are different from the others. Every one of those marks, I want covered in a fucking tattoo. Something beautiful and fierce to remind me I'm not a fucking victim!" I yelled the last part, needing to let more of the rage inside me out so I didn't explode.

"You'll have them, honey. Anything you want. I'll be right there with you. You and me, Serelda. Always you and me."

Brick held me while I cried and grieved. I knew Roman was doing much the same with my sister. I wasn't sure how I was going to be able to look at Winter again without reliving that whole, nasty mess. We'd figure it out because I couldn't live without my sister, but this was insane.

I'm not sure how long we sat in the bathroom, but eventually, I calmed down. Brick stood with me in his arms and sat me on the vanity while he wet a washcloth and washed my face tenderly. Then he fixed my toothbrush and handed it to me. I used it automatically, not knowing what else to do.

When I was finished, he undressed me, then himself, and put us both in the shower. The water was hot, like I needed it. Brick poured shower gel over my body, moving me out of the spray before rubbing my skin with his hands until I was lathered from neck to feet.

"What's Sting going to do with that sadistic bastard?" I couldn't help the question.

"He's going to kill him. Eventually."

"He'll make him suffer?"

"As much as you and Winter want him to. He's the president, and the decision is ultimately his, but I'll ask him to give you that if you want me to. I've never asked him for anything, so I know this is something he'll give me. Just say the word, baby."

"I want him to suffer. If that makes me a bad person, so be it. I want him to suffer so long he begs for death. Then I want him to suffer some more."

"I'll make it happen. It will go on for as long as Sting will let it. He starts lettin' up and thinkin' about lettin' him die, I'll push as hard as I can, Serelda. This will be my gift to you."

I held Brick's gaze for long moments, really thinking about it. "No." I sighed, the last of the immediate anger and pain evaporating. "No. Let Sting take care of him. However he chooses." I shook my head. "He's not worth another second of my time."

"Serelda. My woman." Brick wrapped his arms around me. The water poured over us in a heated fall.

With Brick holding me tight, praising me as he did, I soon relaxed, my mind going blissfully numb. "My brave, brave woman."

"I love you, Xander. I love you so much it hurts, and I never want to be without you."

"You'll never have to. I'll be with you as long as I fuckin' live."

I wrapped my arms around his neck and pulled Brick down for a searing kiss. I tried to put every ounce of feeling I had for him into that kiss. I'd told him I loved him, but I needed to show him. He was everything to me. Brick had come after me. He'd protected me with everything he had. He'd killed for me and promised to use every bit of pull he had in this club to make my nightmare suffer for as long as he could. Brick was the wall between me and everyone else. He was the one man in the whole world who got me. And he was the only man in the world I would ever want with my heart and soul.

Brick let me kiss him over and over, thrusting his tongue into my mouth counter to my own thrusts into his. Fingers threaded into my hair, Brick moved me where he wanted me, though not taking complete control. He seemed to know I needed to lead this encounter. At least, until I didn't. Brick would know when to take over, and he would master me when he did. And I'd love every fucking second of it.

I reached between us as I kissed him, stroking his cock. It was trapped between our wet bodies, and I pressed it against my belly while I rubbed my hand up and down. He groaned, still kissing me, his fingers digging into my back where he held me. I loved the sounds he made when he was turned-on. I loved knowing it was me who'd done this to him.

"Fuck, baby. Just... FUCK!" Brick let his head fall

back as I continued to stroke his cock. It throbbed and pulsed in my hand. Precum leaked from the tip in drop after slick drop. I started to sink to my knees, but Brick tightened his fingers in my hair. "No," he bit out. "Need your pussy, woman."

"Brick!" I cried out as he spun me around and mashed me against the shower frame. One arm was around my waist while the other hand guided his cock into my pussy. The sweet friction was like the most brutal pressure I'd ever imagined. The second he was inside me, Brick wrapped his other arm around me to palm a breast, then started moving.

It wasn't gentle lovemaking. Brick took me over when I needed it most. He drove every sane thought from my head with the most intense, world-shattering sensations. Brick. My rock. My... *everything*.

* * *

Brick

When the storm passed, Serelda put herself in my care. It took time, but I gave her as long as I could. When I couldn't stand the separation any longer, I took her. And she let me.

Serelda gave herself to me so sweetly it nearly brought tears to my eyes. She was so willing to follow where I led her in everything. It was like once she threw her heart into our relationship, she never looked back. She trusted me to take care of her, and that's what I'd do.

I fucked Serelda, growling and grunting with every surge of my body into hers. My lips were at her neck, nipping and licking. I drove her as high as I could with dirty words and soft caresses. When I couldn't hold back any longer, I let one hand slide to her pussy, finding her clit with one finger and circling it over and over until I felt her cunt spasm around my dick.

She screamed my name, her body trembling with the force of her orgasm. Hers triggered mine, and the next thing I knew, I was coming deep inside Serelda while I bellowed to the ceiling.

We stayed like that for a while, catching our breath. My cock was still embedded inside her, though growing soft. I reached for the shower gel and cleaned her carefully, not wanting her to be uncomfortable when I took her to bed. She was limp in my arms as I carried her from the shower. Once again, I sat her on the vanity while I dried her. I knew there was no sense in dressing her. I planned on taking her all night long until she was so drained she passed out.

"I got you, baby."

"Brick…" She rested her head on my chest while I finished drying her before closing my arms around her and holding her for precious seconds.

"Ready for bed?"

"Yeah. You'll stay with me?" Her voice was husky from screaming, and she was drooping where she sat. Hopefully, she'd sleep for a couple hours before waking. But when she did, I'd be ready. If things went the way I wanted them to, we'd be in this room for at least a couple of days. By that time, maybe the sharpness of her grief would have dulled. I knew she'd insist on talking to Sting soon, but I thought I could keep her occupied long enough for my president to do what needed doing.

"Absolutely. I will not leave this room without you, Serelda. Not for any reason. I need anything, I'll have a prospect bring it. If that's not possible, I'll take you with me. But I will not leave you alone."

"Thank you."

"Anything you need, baby, I'll provide."

I carried her to the bed and pulled her against me, her head on my shoulder, her fingers digging into my side as she clung to me.

"I love you, baby. Love you so fuckin' much."

"I love you too. Thanks for redirecting me. I needed the outlet for my anger, but I don't ever want to dwell on this evening again. It's done. The nightmare's over."

"It is, baby. You're safe. Just so you know, I'll always slay your monsters. You just point me in the right direction."

"Thanks for giving me back my self-esteem. I know now what it means to live. I'll never be in the shadows again."

"No. You won't. You're my woman. My fierce, proud, warrior woman. Mine."

"Yours." Serelda took one last, deep breath, sighed contentedly, then fell asleep with a smile on her face, and my heart in her hands. She was the woman for me. The only woman I'd ever loved. I'd protect her until my dying day and relish every fucking second.

My woman.

My world.

My… Serelda.

Marteeka Karland

Erotic romance author by night, emergency room tech/clerk by day, Marteeka Karland works really hard to drive everyone in her life completely and totally nuts. She has been creating stories from her warped imagination since she was in the third grade. Her love of writing blossomed throughout her teenage years until it developed into the totally unorthodox and irreverent style her English teachers tried so hard to rid her of.

Bones MC Multiverse
- Bones MC
- Salvation's Bane MC
- Shadow Demons
- Black Reign MC
- Iron Tzars MC

Marteeka at Changeling: changelingpress.com/marteeka-karland-a-39

Changeling Press E-Books

More Sci-Fi, Fantasy, Paranormal, and BDSM adventures available in e-book format for immediate download at ChangelingPress.com -- Werewolves, Vampires, Dragons, Shapeshifters and more -- Erotic Tales from the edge of your imagination.

What are E-Books?

E-books, or electronic books, are books designed to be read in digital format -- on your desktop or laptop computer, notebook, tablet, Smart Phone, or any electronic e-book reader.

Where can I get Changeling Press E-Books?

Changeling Press e-books are available at ChangelingPress.com, Amazon, Apple Books, Barnes & Noble, Kobo, Smashwords, and other retailers.

ChangelingPress.com

Printed in Great Britain
by Amazon